ANOTHER GOVERNESS

THE LEAST BLACKSMITH

ANOTHER GOVERNESS

THE LEAST BLACKSMITH

A DIPTYCH

JOANNA RUOCCO

FOREWORD BY BEN MARCUS

TUSCALOOSA

Copyright © 2012 by Joanna Ruocco
The University of Alabama Press
Tuscaloosa, Alabama 35487-0380
All rights reserved
Manufactured in the United States of America

Book Design: Illinois State University's English Department's Publications
Unit; Director: Tara Reeser; Assistant Director: Steve Halle; Production
Assistant: Aida Giurgianu
Cover Design: Lou Robinson
Typefaces: Caslon Pro and Garamond

⊗

The paper on which this book is printed meets the minimum requirements
of American National Standard for Information Sciences—Permanence
of Paper for Printed Library Materials, ANSI Z39.48–1984.

Library of Congress Cataloging-in-Publication Data
Ruocco, Joanna.
    Another governess ; The least blacksmith : a diptych / Joanna Ruocco ;
foreword by Ben Marcus. — 1st ed.
        p. cm.
    ISBN 978-1-57366-165-2 (quality paper : alk. paper) — ISBN 978-1-
57366-829-3 (electronic)
    I. Ruocco, Joanna. Least blacksmith. II. Title.
    PS3618.U568A84 2012
    813'.6—dc23
                                    2011043108

For my namesakes

TABLE OF CONTENTS

FOREWORD

by Ben Marcus

What marks this severe book is an astounding level of discipline in the prose. Joanna Ruocco, a writer of stark effects, seems to have squeezed her sentences so tightly they are sheer muscle. Just read a few. They are simple, strict, rarely veering from the basic structure you might encounter in a children's book. I thought of the Dick and Jane books, the sing-song cadence of simple factual lines. But this is no children's book. What starts out innocently almost always veers into strangeness or violence. Ruocco does something wonderful here. She builds writing sentence by sentence until, by force of logic, she achieves a genuine discomfort. This is a literary discomfort, borne of that same discipline in the prose. One senses that perhaps Ruocco worked from a deliberately limited vocabulary. Certain words appear with regularity: cakes, glass, fluid, lump, glue, blood, dogs, moat, nits, butcher. She shuffles these words while remaining obedient to her narrative—and there is a beguiling, grisly, poignant narrative here (actually, there are many)—and somehow, through this deliberate practice, meaning grows, a world blooms, a story emerges. It's part fairy tale, part gothic, part domestic, and wholly its own odd species of writing. Listen:

> She must be like the mistress, red and fat like the mistress. There is no mistress. I would know if there were a mistress, a red, fat mistress. A mistress does not tolerate offal on the staircase, flies and hornets on the staircase. She does not tolerate boils on the meat. The mistress has gone away from the house. She is buried beneath the tree in the garden by the house. She is buried too deep to come up. The dogs cannot reach her.

A violence is suggested here, but the effect is punishingly flat. Ruocco seems to go out of her way not to provide the usual assistance of adverbs and adjectives. Thank god. Without the symphonic soundtrack meant to telegraph feeling, we have only the haunted content itself, bravely stripped of cues and signals. What I most appreciate here is the sense of tremendous control on display. If these are strange narrative waters, if we are in the hands of an artist determined to navigate her own way, taking nothing for granted in the literary toolkit, we experience Ruocco's sheer control through every sentence, the comforting feeling that she has designed this book not as a container for self-expression, but as a piece of linguistic architecture that could not possibly have been built any other way. This strikes me as the brilliant, ideal approach to literary innovation, and it makes me surrender fully to the gorgeous, original world of Ruocco's narratives. It is so easy to submit to a writer who has this much power—we know there is nothing capricious or random here—and if we are unmoored or delirious or just unsure of what is happening, it is only for a moment, and that confusion turns out to be deliberate, in service of the dark art of this writing. Finishing this book, I thought: I must read everything this writer has written. And: I must tell people that the project of literature is in not just capable hands, but unusual, original ones.

ANOTHER GOVERNESS

1

My hair is altogether changed. My face is altogether changed. I am very slim. The dress hangs on me. It slides from my shoulder and the cloth is newly stained. A button dangles. I must repair the button. There is a needle in the nursery. Somewhere there is a needle. I will use it to repair the button. There are children in the nursery. The grunting is the children, the sounds of the children. The children are grunting over the tray of cakes. On the iron table, a big tray of cakes, little cakes, dripping cakes. There are two children grunting over the big tray of cakes. They are on their knees by the cakes. The girl has reddish eyelids and nostrils. The boy is swollen, with dirty skin. Tamworth and Old Spot. I will call them Tamworth and Old Spot. The boy is nearly a man. Spot is a man. The children are grown. They are not children. They are on their knees. That is why they look so small. No one has noticed they are grown because they eat on their knees. Get up, I say to the children. Get up. Get up. The children grunt. Crumbs stick to their cheeks. They move closer to the tray. There are more cakes on the tray. There are more cakes for the children to eat. Get up, I say. Get up. Get up. I clap my hands. The children look up. They stare. Crumbs drop from their mouths. Fluids drip down their chins. They stare. I stand above them in the nursery so they know me even if they do not know my face.

2

I walk in a small circle on the carpet. Fluids have marked the carpet. I walk in small circles. There is a table in the nursery. There are two chairs. There is a rocking horse. The paint has chipped from the legs of the rocking horse and the tail is ragged, falling short of the fetlocks. Something has chewed the legs, chewed the tail of the rocking horse. Nits fly from the eggs in the gapped mane of the rocking horse. Nits swarm above the crib. I walk to the crib. It is iron. I walk to the rocking horse. Ride on your rocking horse, I say to Spot, but he is too big for the rocking horse. His legs will bend at the knee, his feet on the carpet. He does not ride the rocking horse. There must be another child, a small child, under the linens in the crib. I walk to the window. I look down at the moat. There is a dirty white skin of mist on the moat. Beyond the moat the orchard thickens into the forest. The orchard is filled with pigs. The pigs are shoulder to shoulder, feeding in the orchard. The apples are soft and brown. They are dropping from the trees. They are rotting in the grass. The pigs are slipping in the thick brown flesh of the apples, the broken flesh of the apples. The brown skins of the apples hang in flaps from their bellies. The pigs nip at each other, squealing. The pigs are eating through the apples to the soil. They are eating through the soil. A pig drags a root from the soil, a pale, streaked root, long and stiff, tapered to a white hook. The pig is eating the white root and the root is moistening, blackening with fluids. I croon to the pigs. The pigs must think that they smell me beneath the soil, but I am behind the glass in the high window. I am high above the orchard. I will not go back there anymore. I have misted the window with my breath.

3

Open your books, I say. The children certainly have books. The nursery is filled with books. I see books on the desks by bottles of black fluid and I see books on the carpet. The crib is filled with books. There are no books on the table. On the table, there are cakes. The children wait by the cakes, on their knees by the cakes. It is not time for cakes. It is time for books. First, in the nursery, cakes. Then books. It is time for books. Not all little children have books. Tamworth and Spot must love their books. There is much to learn in their books. There are no books in the forest. I went to the forest. There were roots, there were rocks, there were leaves. There was mud. I fell in the mud. I slid in the leaves. I crawled over rocks. I lay in a field. I cut a lump on my foot and a worm came out. It was a very black worm. I dried my foot in the sun. There was a hole in the lump on my foot, and the hole leaked yellow fluid. I pulled dark strings from the hole with my fingernails. Pinched between my fingernails, the dark strings did not wiggle. I thought they were worms, but they did not wiggle. They were not worms. I rolled them hard between my fingers. They did not smear. They remained tiny dark strings. They were moist and they left no color on my skin. They were something, not worms or blood, a third thing that worms and blood made together in the lump on my foot. I hobbled to the low stone wall. I lay on top of the low stone wall. I thought about the dark strings in the lump on my foot. They were moving up my legs. I felt them behind my knees. They dammed and swelled in the crook of my arm, under my lower eyelids, curling around and around. I wrapped my foot with canvas that crusted with the yellow fluid. My foot smelled in its canvas wrapper. The farmer held me close then pushed me away. What is that smell? said the farmer. His face was pink, with white hairs, and his mouth was a ragged wet hole like the hole in my foot. My foot, I said, because I knew what smell the farmer meant. Open your foot, I say to the children. I laugh. The children have not noticed that I limp, that I drag myself across the carpet in circles, as though I fall, but every time I fall, I catch myself. I keep moving.

4

The baker had a daughter. The baker's daughter worked in the bakery. She cut the gray cakes of yeast. She mixed yeast and water for the baker. Her fingers were wrinkled with moisture and they gave off a sour odor. The nails had come loose in the nail beds. The skin that seals the nails in the nail beds was too soft to hold the nails in place. One day a man cut a loaf of bread and he found a string of hair. The string of hair passed lengthwise through the bread from end to end. The baker cut the hairs from the daughter's head. One day a man cut a loaf of bread and he found ten fingernails in the center of the loaf of bread. The baker cut the daughter's fingers at the first knuckles. One day a man cut a loaf of bread and he found the key to the bakery. The man did not tell the baker. The man came in the night to the bakery where the baker's daughter waited. The baker's daughter showed the man the sack of coins the baker hid beneath the floorboard and the man lifted out the sack of coins. He lifted the skirt around the waist of the baker's daughter and felt with his fingers beneath the skirt. His fingernails were ragged and the baker's daughter cried out so that the man put his forearm across her mouth. The baker's daughter did not cry out again. The baker was upstairs sleeping in his narrow bed. The man dropped one of the baker's coins on the floor for the baker's daughter. The next day a man cut a loaf of bread and he found a coin in the heel of the bread. The baker crushed his daughter's skull with the whetting stone. He put her beneath the floorboard in a sack.

5

The children eat and eat. The children cannot stop eating. They cannot stop while there are cakes on the tray. Even as they chew their cakes they shove more cakes into their mouths. Spot gags. He keeps chewing. He gags. Spit, I say to Spot. I put my hand below his mouth. Spit, I say. I put my fingers on his lips. The teeth are moving up and down, and the lips. The lips are wet and bits of cake cling to my fingers. My fingers are moving up and down on the lips. I want to push my fingers through Spot's lips and pull out the cake. I can see the cake between the teeth, the wet ball of cake, and the tongue swelling, and then the tongue jerks forward and the wet ball of cake rises. The wet ball of cake comes forward, comes through the teeth. It bulges through the lips. It hangs on the lips. I push the cake back into the mouth. Spot gags. I laugh. Spot reaches for another cake. Stop, I say to Spot. Spot looks at me. He pushes the cake through his lips. I push my finger through his lips. I feel the teeth. The teeth are hard in the wetness of the mouth. Ribs are hard in the wetness of the chest. I stepped between the ribs, the soft large bulge that rose between the ribs. She had lain in the field in the sun and the rain. For a moment, my foot pressed the surface, then the surface gave way. My foot pushed through the surface. There was a sound, the sound of the air going out. It smelled bad. My foot entered the cavity. Inside, it was wet. I felt the wetness seething on my skin. Her dress hung in a bush. Her dress flapped in the wind, threads caught in the thorns of the bush. A button dangled. There is no needle in the forest. I could not repair the button. It was a nice dress, stiffened with fluids. The rain could not wash the fluids from the dress. I could wash the dress in the river, the clean, cold river. I could beat the dress on the rocks. I did not want to bend too close. I did not push with my finger. I opened her lips with a stick. Her mouth was filled with fluids. She was very plump. She ate cakes with the children, cake after cake. The cakes turned to fluids in her mouth, or her mouth was open all night. Her mouth filled with rain.

6

There is a tray of cakes on the table. There is a pitcher of milk.
Spot drinks from the pitcher. He coughs into the pitcher. Milk
runs down Spot's chin as he puts the pitcher on the table. He
lets the milk drip. He reaches for a cake. I should stop him.
The cakes will sicken the children. The cook used bad flour.
There is alum in the wheat. There is chalk in the wheat. The
cook mixed rancid fat with the flour. She worked the fat and
flour in the trough. Sweat ran down her arms. The air was hot
and thick. The cook grunted. She could not see the changes to
my hair and face. Not through the hot, thick air. In the kitch-
en, there is smoke in the air. There is soot in the air. There
are flies in the air. I crouched by the trough. Lower down,
the smoke clears. There is less smoke by the trough. I put my
face in the trough. It smelled bad. Beneath the trough, something scurried. The cook put her heel down hard. She grunted.
She scraped her heel on the edge of the table leg. Something

dropped. The cook rubbed fat into the sores on her arms. She did not notice how I breathed with my face in the trough, how I gagged on the rancid smell from the trough. I crouch beside the table with the children. I break off a piece of cake and put it in my mouth. My mouth is dry. The cake comes apart. I breathe carefully, but the bits of cake fly against the back of my throat. I gag. My mouth itches. My tongue has grown fine white hairs like the hairs on Spot's cheeks. Fine white hairs cluster on my tongue. I turn my back to the children to scrape at my tongue with my nails.

7

It is a grand house. There are many rooms, closed rooms, locked rooms. The nursery is a closed room. It is a locked room. There is a key to the nursery. She had a key. She must have had a key. She locked the children in the room. Otherwise the children would crawl down the halls. They would hide in the shadows in the halls, behind the paintings in the halls, between the drapes, beneath the rugs. In a grand house, it is hard to hunt the children. The halls go on and on. The fireplaces have enormous mouths, deep black mouths. I would hurry down the halls. I would listen for the grunting in the drapes. I would sniff beneath the rugs. Where are the children? I would say. Where are the children? The children do not leave the nursery. They crouch by the table. They crawl to the corners. They make their mess in the corners. The carpet is marked with fluids. It is wet with fluids. The fluids have made marks on the walls. The children make their mess against the walls, against the door of the nursery. They scratch at the door. Their fluids spread to the other side of the door. Their fluids spread through the halls. The smell of the children fills the grand house. The cook smells the nursery from the kitchen. It is stronger than the smell that rises from the trough, than the smell that hangs between the buzzing meats above her head.

8

My shoes are very large. They gape around my ankles. The soles are rimmed with offal. I have tracked the offal on the carpet in the nursery. The children have noticed the offal, the smell of the offal. They have felt the thicker offal where it smears into the slickness of the fluids. They slip on the offal when they crawl around the table on their knees. I did not intend to track offal on the carpet in the nursery. The smell in the nursery is strengthened by the offal. I must have stepped in offal on the staircase. The dogs drag the offal to the staircase. Flies crawl on the offal. Hornets crawl on the offal. The housekeeper should shovel the offal from the staircase. In a grand house, there is too much for the housekeeper to do. The fabric of the curtains makes dust. The paper on the walls makes dust. The hairs on the dogs make dust. The dust piles up higher and higher. The dust makes the housekeeper weep. She coughs. She weeps. She moves weeping through the rooms. She coughs on the dust. She weeps on the dust. I hear fluids in her cough. Fluids fall on the dust. They wet the dust. The housekeeper makes sludge. She makes mud. Mud is better than dust. Dust gets inside your nose. It gets inside your mouth. It gets inside your eyes. It makes your mouth spit. It makes your eyes weep. You have mud on your chin, said the farmer. He dropped a rag on my face. The housekeeper wipes mud with a rag. She empties pails. She cleans the high windows in the tower. She looks down at the orchard. The housekeeper sees what happens in the orchard. She sees through the clean windows. She sees the pigs, she sees the dogs. She sees between the black boughs of the trees, long pale hair. My hair is dark. Dark and short. My face is very long. If the housekeeper were to see me, creeping from the orchard, she would not let me near the nursery. She would run from the tower, around and around down the tower, through hall after hall. She would pull her shovel from the offal and block the staircase with her shovel. I would try to hide my dark hair with my hands. I would try to ascend. I would hide my long face with my hair. I would hide my hair with my hands. Up the staircase, the hall leads to the nursery. There is a needle in the nursery, an embroidery needle. There must be an embroidery needle. Girls must learn to embroider. With an embroidery needle, I could embroider a border of flowers on the dress. I could repair the button on the dress. The button dangles. It would go poorly with a border of flowers. I should be able to explain about the button. I should be able to explain about the border. I must have a needle, I would say, through my hair, through my hands. I am wanting a needle. The housekeeper would hear that my voice is changed. She would strike me with her shovel, sever my neck with the edge of her shovel. I will push the housekeeper, but I will slip. I will slip down the staircase. I will slip on the offal. I will bleed from my neck. My head will fall forward and my head will fall back. My chin is wet. My chest is wet. I run into the curtains. I run into the wall. My head falls back. I see the room upside down. Blood runs up my nose. Blood runs over the lower lids of my eyes. The housekeeper is red. Her shovel is red. I fit my hands inside my neck, all ten knuckles in my neck, but blood comes around my knuckles. My head falls forward. I get on my knees. I put my hands on the floor. I put my head on the floor. The dust makes me cough. I spit blood on the floor. I thicken the dust. I stir with my hands. The dust is thicker and thicker. I swallow blood with my mouth and it comes out my neck. It wets my chin. It wets my chest. I crawl with my head on the floor and push my face through the mud. I sink up to my chest in the mud. In the swamp, the mud is red. Smiths cut the mud. They put the mud in carts. They take the carts to the furnace. They heat the mud. They hammer the mud. They beat the mud until nothing can break it. The mud is black and not red.

9

There is dust in the air. There are nits in the air. There is dirt on the windows. The light is dim. It is dirty, dim light. The children think my hair is pale, long and pale, darkened by the dirty, dim light. They think my face is just a sliver in the light. I crowd the children from the table. I eat cake after cake. The cakes are not good. They make a hard lump in my belly. I can feel the lump through the dress. I am very slim. I am very straight and very slim, but now there is a lump, an ugly, bad lump. I squeeze the lump. I twist the lump. Lift up your shirt, I say to Spot. He lifts up his shirt. I press his belly. I feel a hard lump. Spot grunts. It is the cakes. The cakes are not good. The cook scraped the paper from the walls to mix with the wheat. There is dye on the paper. There is glue on the paper. There is plaster on the paper and white hairs from the lath. The cook has damaged the walls. Without the paper, plaster cracks. It crumbles. The cook has made holes in the walls. The plaster spills on the floor. The cook tracks plaster through the house. She has tracked plaster through the nursery. I see white powder on the carpet. I see white powder on the cakes. I see hairs in the powder. I take the tray of cakes and walk to the window. No, says Tamworth. No. No. She crawls behind me too slowly. I reach the window. I strike the dim glass with the tray. The glass cracks. Light comes through the crack. I make a hole in the glass with the corner of the tray. Light comes through the hole. I push a cake through the hole, but the cake crumbles. Crumbs stick to the glass. I push the cake harder. Blood runs on the glass. I leave the one cake smashed in the window. I say, There is glass in the cakes. I laugh. Tamworth lies facedown on the carpet, arms reaching toward the window. I walk around Tamworth. I put the tray on the table. Spot leans forward. He shoves a cake in his mouth. His shirt is pushed up. He smiles with the cake in his mouth. He rests his hand on his belly. I move his hand. While he chews, I press the lump in his belly. It is the size of an apple. The apple moves up and down as he chews. Who gave you the apple? I say. My hand leaves a brown stain on the lump on Spot's belly. It is very like an apple. Here is your apple, I say to Tamworth. I hold Spot's arms. He does not move. Tamworth crawls toward us. She rises to her knees. She puts her mouth on Spot's lump. She opens her mouth on the lump. She roots in Spot's belly for the apple. Spot grunts, but he does not move. He has little red bumps on his arms. He has white hairs on his cheeks. His skin is wet. It smells bad. I hold him against the dress. His sweat softens the stains on my dress.

10

Spot is grown. He is a man. The Master must be an old man, a very old man. I did not realize the Master was such an old man. The Master walks with a stick. He beats the floor with the stick. He beats the walls with the stick. We hear his cries and the blows of the stick. We hear the Master on the stairs. We hear the Master in the hall. We hear the Master pass the door. Spot crawls toward the door. Tamworth crawls after. Master, says Spot, but the Master does not stop. He is going up to the tower, around and around the spiral steps to the tower. From the tower, the Master can see what happens in the orchard. He can see through the black boughs of the apple trees. He can see through the black boughs and into the black brush of the forest, the bushes and brambles, the mud and the rocks and the leaves. He can see the shapes crawling like lice in the forest, even through the milk on his eyes.

11

The brickmaker had a daughter. She lived by the beck, hard by the beck. She lived alone by the beck. The brickmaker worked in the brickfield and his daughter lived by the beck. The brickmaker made bricks with refuse and clay. He mixed one part refuse to five parts clay. The beck had a stone bed and between the stones, clay. When the brickmaker's daughter pried up the stones to scoop the clay, the water clouded. The water clouded gray blue and the clouds thinned in the currents of the beck, carried downstream in the beck, gray blue streaks in the beck stretching down to the village at the bottom of the gorge. The brickmaker's daughter scooped the clay into a bucket. She carried the bucket to the brickfield. To get to the brickfield, she passed through the village. The brickmaker's daughter followed the beck through the village and every now and then she clouded the water with a handful of clay. One day the billposter saw the brickmaker's daughter veer from the beck. She veered from the beck with her bucket. She crossed through the churchyard. She stopped by the bakery, by the open ditch by the coal heap by the bakery. She put down her bucket. The open ditch was narrow and the brickmaker's daughter stood with one foot on either side of the ditch. She stood astride the ditch with her skirt hanging down and she made water into the ditch. She picked up her bucket and she returned to the beck, to the black bank of the beck that flowed through the village to the brickfield. She followed the beck. From then on, the billposter watched for the brickmaker's daughter. The brickmaker's daughter came down the steep path toward the village with her bucket. She passed through the village. She braced the bucket on her hip, or she tilted the bucket forward so the base of the bucket rested on her thigh. Sometimes she veered. She veered from the beck to the bakery. She made her water, upright, astride the open ditch by the coal heap by the bakery. Finally, the billposter could not contain his curiosity. He came out from behind the tree where he had been pretending to post his bills. Let me carry your heavy bucket, said the billposter. He had a black beard and he smiled through the black beard at the brickmaker's daughter. He lifted her bucket from where she had set it on the coal heap and he carried her bucket to the beck. He followed the beck to the brickfield and the brickmaker's daughter followed behind. When they arrived at the ridge overlooking the brickfield, the billposter put down the bucket. He sat on a stone and he pulled the brickmaker's daughter across his knees. He tickled her ear. He folded up her skirt and inspected her buttocks. Her buttocks bore a mark, two white protuberances, like the paps of a ewe. The billposter struck a tack into the larger protuberance with his long-handled hammer. The skin broke but did not bleed. The brickmaker's daughter grunted. Struggling, she stretched out her hands. She pulled the rim of the bucket. She tipped the bucket and her hands sank into the clay in the bucket. The billposter lifted her from his knees and she stood before him, upright, with her gray blue hands hanging down at her sides. Clouds had thickened in the sky. The billposter felt as though he were being pressed into the stone and grew afraid. He rose and moved forward. He pushed the brickmaker's daughter so that she toppled backwards from the ridge. She landed below on the brickfield. Her impact forced the gray blue moisture up through the earth and the gray blue moisture lay like a stain on the earth around the brickmaker's daughter. The billposter picked up the bucket. He emptied the bucket onto the brickfield from the ridge so that the brickmaker could mix the clay with the refuse and so fill his wagon with bricks.

12

I dip the hem of my dress in the pitcher of milk. I clean the skin on my face. I pick between my teeth. I pick beneath my nails. I am pretty and clean. I squeeze gray milk from the hem of my dress. I straighten my dress. I am pretty and clean for the lesson. Spot notices that I am clean. He stands on his feet, his big feet. He totters. He walks toward me. He lifts his shirt. It hurts, says Spot. He puts my hand on the lump. He whimpers. He moves my hand back and forth on the lump. He comes closer. He is very tall, very thick and tall. On his feet, he looks grown. He bends his neck and rests his brow on the top of my head. He breathes on my face, my pretty, clean face. Spot is tall. He is grown, but I can tell that he is hardly a man. His breath is wet. His breath smells spoiled, sweet and spoiled. Around the hard lump, his belly is soft. The buttons on my dress sink into his belly. Black buttons disappear in his belly. Sometimes there are currants in cakes, black currants sunk in the cake.

There is a lesson about black currant cake. Two girls ate a black currant cake. They spread cloth napkins on their dresses. They put their hats on the grasses. They lifted the wedges of cake with their hands. They were great big girls. They flattened the grasses. Their teeth turned black. They laughed. They picked each other's teeth. They licked each other's teeth so the teeth were white and clean. They spread cream on the cake. They put their blackened fingers in cream. There are lessons in the nursery. There is so much to learn. I work my fingers between Spot's belly and the buttons. My fingers get wet. They slide on Spot's skin. I bend my fingers so my nails dig in Spot's skin. Spot does not act like a man. He whines. The fluid from his lips drops on my face. Go to your desk, I say. I poke with my fingers. I jerk with my head so Spot's brow slips and his face comes down fast. He takes a big step so he does not fall. He lifts his head. His chin is wet and he does not shut his mouth. He does not smile. Go to your desk, I say. In the corner of the room, there are two desks. Each desk has its bottle of fluid. Each desk has its pile of books. I walk to the desks. Tamworth is crouching beneath a desk. She puts her hands on her knees and looks between her legs. She makes her mess beneath the desk. Her legs shake. She looks at me.

13

On the desks, the books are black. The spines are black. The covers are black. I open the books. Inside, I see black. The children have ripped the pages from the books. I lift a book by its spine. The covers tap together. I make the edges of the covers tap together. The book has black jaws. I laugh. How will the children read the books? I nip Tamworth's arm with the book. I nip her shoulder. I nip Tamworth's nose with the book. She laughs. She knocks the book from my hands. The jaws fall open. The Master's dogs have black, speckled gums. The Master's dogs are old. Their teeth are worn low in their gums. The Master's dogs have stiffened in their hips. Their back legs are stiff when they run. The Master's dogs make their mess in the orchard. They cannot crouch. They make their mess like cows in the field. They lift their tails. They run through the orchard, their mess falling behind. Their mess is yellow fluids. I could not wipe it from the apples. The skins on the apples are cracked. The fluids seeped beneath the skins. The Master's dogs leak fluid in the house. The Master lets his dogs in every room of the house. The nursery door is locked from the outside. The dogs inside the nursery have been inside for a very long time. The children have scattered the piles of hair.

14

There are two chairs in the nursery. The children sit on the chairs. I sit on the rocking horse. The rocking horse creaks. I am very slim, but it creaks. Dust falls from the withers. Nits rise from the withers. I sit astride the rocking horse. The saddle is hard. I tighten my legs. The saddle rubs. It hurts. I lean forward and back. I make the rocking horse creak. The hips have stiffened. The hips creak. The legs are very straight. Nits swarm around the nostrils of the rocking horse. Nits lay their eggs in the nostrils. They crawl between the lips. Tamworth feeds the rocking horse cake. She crumbles cakes in her palm and presses her palm on the lips. She fills the gouge between the lips with cake. She fills the nostrils with cake. Now mess, says Tamworth. She puts her mouth by the ear. Mess, says Tamworth. Nits settle on her cheeks and she slaps the nits. Her cheeks blotch. She tugs the mane with her fist. She slaps the neck. She slaps my leg. Make him mess, says Tamworth.

She puts her hand on my neck. She pulls my dress. She tries to sit astride the horse. I push her back. Mess, says Tamworth. She slaps the haunch of the rocking horse. She lifts the tail of the rocking horse. I stand up and the rocking horse rocks forward and back. The withers bump my sex. It hurts. Blood is running through Tamworth's mouth where the hindquarters pushed her lips against her teeth.

15

The children eat and mess. The dogs eat and mess. The Master eats. He messes. There are pails for the Master's messes all through the house. Only the rocking horse does not mess. The food stays in the mouth and nostrils of the rocking horse. It greens. It hatches nits. In the kitchen, the cook takes meat from the hooks. The cook shaves the coating that forms on the meat, the green coating that forms on the meat. On the hooks, the meat grows boils. It buzzes. The cook digs out the boils with a very thin knife. She chews a sprig of fresh mint. She rubs mint on the meat. She freshens the meat. The Master likes the fresh meat. In a grand house, the Master eats meat every day. He eats meat from white plates. That is mint jelly on the meat. It is fresh. There is a white pot of sugar. He sugars the meat. No, he sugars the tea. He likes the tea very sweet, very sweet and white with fresh milk. The brown tea turns white. The children eat cakes in the nursery. They grow. They need to eat and eat. They eat. They drink milk. They make their mess. They eat. They mess. They are good children. They tear the pages from the books. They use the pages to clean what remains of their mess. They clean their bodies from what remains of their mess. They clean their bodies. Spot is a man. He can clean his own body. The torn pages of the books are crumpled in the corners. Spot is not like a pig. He is not like a dog. He is good and clean. He is like the Master. I see now that he is like the Master, very like the Master. He belongs in the grand house. Tamworth is not like the Master. She must be like the Mistress, red and fat like the Mistress. There is no Mistress. I would know if there were a Mistress, a red, fat Mistress. A Mistress does not tolerate offal on the staircase, flies and hornets on the staircase. She does not tolerate boils on the meat. The Mistress has gone away from the house. She is buried beneath the tree in the garden by the house. She is buried too deep to come up. The dogs cannot reach her.

16

Where is your globe? says Spot. Yes, says Tamworth. Her jaws move slowly. A cake rests in her mouth. She lets her jaws hang. Spot's face is moist. Spot stands. He is very large. His legs quiver. The fabric of his trousers is too thin. I see the shapes beneath the fabric and the stains on the surface of the fabric. Tamworth rubs the redness of her lids and nose, the webs of veins that raise the skin on her lids and nose. It is not time for books, says Spot. It is time for globes. Spot's eyes are moist. They are brighter. He watches me closely. The Master is near. The Master is in the hall. He paces the hall. We hear him pass. We hear him pass. Spot jerks with each blow of the stick down the hall. He jerks. His legs quiver. He lifts his fat hand and pokes the dirty skin of his face. He pulls a white thread from the corner of his mouth. He puts the thread on his trousers. He watches me closely. He is standing. He is taller than I am. He is wider than I am. Your hair is black, says Spot. Today your hair is black. You have forgotten your globe. I turn my back on Tamworth and Spot. I face the door. I face the crib. I face the rocking horse. I want to sit down, but I will not sit on the rocking horse. I do not have a globe. I have a dress. I have a ribbon. I have stockings and shoes. The dress hangs on me. A button dangles. A globe is a map, says Spot. A round map. A map is flat. A flat map. Find the nursery on the map, I say. The nursery is not flat. It is not round. The nursery is neither flat nor round. The nursery is a shape, I say. Spot takes Tamworth by the neck. He drags her from the chair. He pushes an arm between her legs. He lifts and Tamworth twists. She hops. Spot drags her around the crib. He hits Tamworth's head on the leg of the crib. The crib does not move. A sound comes from the crib. A short sound. Above the crib there is a map. The map is on the wall. Spot has thrown food at the map. Tamworth has thrown food at the map. Porridge has wetted the map. White tea has wetted the map. I walk to the map. Where is the nursery? I say. Find the nursery on the map. The grand house is not on the map. The moat is not on the map. Where is the orchard? I say. Where is the forest? Where is the river? Where are the farmer's fields? Spot points to the map. He says the name of the town. He points to a spot on the map. He says the name of the town. No, I say. That is not the town. That is not the middle of the town, the hot middle of the town, the dusty middle of the town. I did not stand there, on that spot, in the town. The spot is wrong. There is no road on the map. There is no ditch on the map. There is no fire on the map, the fire where the bone boiler sets his pot, where the fat rises to the top of the pot. I skimmed the fat from the water in the pot. I ate the fat. The fat was fresh and hot with a good salt taste. The bone boiler struck me on the face with the flat of the knife. He struck my neck with the flat of the knife. I saw the knife turn over. I saw the flat of the knife. I saw the edge of the knife. I lifted my skirt. The ditch was deep. The river was high. I walked through the river. I held my skirt higher than the river. I slept in a malt barn. I slept in barley rushes on the floor of the malt barn. It smelled sweet. I could hear the bone boiler on the road. I could hear his dogs on the road. I put barley rushes between my legs. They prickled. I put barley rushes between my legs so the dogs would not smell me. I felt the prickle of the rushes. The light came through the cracks in the weatherboards. The sun rose. The light came through the weatherboards. It was cold in the malt barn and I drew my arms inside my dress and folded them tight against my body so my arms pressed against my breasts. I did not like the feel of my arms against my breasts. The dress is too big. It hangs on me. I can easily slip my arms inside. I draw my arms inside. I shut my eyes. I touch my breasts. I do not like the feel of my fingers on my breasts. Beneath the smell of the nursery, I smell the sweetness of the malt barn. I open my eyes. I look at the spot on the map. I touch the curded teats on my breasts. They lengthen. They prickle.

17

To be the Master you must have dogs. You must be surrounded by dogs. Dogs follow the Master. They run ahead of the Master. They feed from his hand. The Master beats his dogs with a stick. They limp. Their legs are straight and stiff. They leak fluid behind. From their jaws, they leak offal. They lick the Master's hand. They come in and out of the house. They go up and down the staircase. They go back and forth across the moat, across the bridge on the moat. They carry offal in their mouths. A Mistress does not allow dogs in the house. Above the Mistress, a marble bench. There is a marble bench. There are pocks in the bench, cysts in the bench. Things wiggle from the cysts. Fat white things. They leave black spots on the bench, black spores on the bench. The garden smells. The dogs chew the grass. They vomit the grass. The garden is slick with the grass that has passed through the dogs. Slick grass piles on the dirt. The gardener has planted lilies on the Mistress. Red lilies.

There are red lilies on the Mistress, going brown in the damp. The Master comes in and out of the house. He does not walk to the garden, through the arched gate to the garden, to sit on the marble bench on the Mistress in the garden, to pick the red lilies that grow tall in the garden. The Master crosses the moat. He enters the orchard. He stares back at the house, at the towers of the house. He does not notice the pigs in the orchard, the pigs running from his dogs in the orchard, the dogs with their jaws on the pigs in the orchard. He does not smell the rotting apples. He does not smell the blood of the pigs. He does not smell the offal. He takes down his trousers. He kneels and the dogs come around. He does not cover himself when his dogs come around. He lies back. He puts his hands on the hairs where they thicken. The dogs hang their heads. They pant. Their tongues come close. The Master lies back. I could creep to the Master. He looks back at the house, where I will be someday, near him.

18

The butcher had a daughter. The butcher worked in the back of the shop and the butcher's daughter worked in the front of the shop. When people passed the shop, it was the butcher's daughter they saw through the window. Everywhere the butcher's daughter went the townspeople recognized her from the butcher shop, but if they saw the butcher they did not know him, except that the butcher's nails were black, because blood had dried beneath the butcher's nails, and the butcher had a thick pad of skin on his thumb from always chopping with the heavy knife. The townspeople did not connect the butcher's face with the butcher shop. Instead, it was the butcher's daughter that they pictured when they thought of the butcher shop. The butcher's daughter was a very black girl, black eyes and hair and she laughed so that the dark inside of her mouth was always visible and her large dark lips covered her white teeth. Men made special trips past the butcher shop to look at the butcher's daughter. Other girls in the town were very black but none of them caused the men to make special trips just to look through the window at the darkness inside their big, wide mouths. One day, an old woman bought a calf's liver from the butcher shop and died. When the townspeople thought about the bad liver that killed the old woman, they pictured the butcher's daughter and they could not be so angry anymore. The butcher's daughter was a very black, very merry girl and the townspeople connected her face with the butcher shop and her dark and full body that the men liked to look at through the butcher shop window, and they were not so angry about the death of the old woman. In the back of the shop, the butcher cut the meat and in the front of the shop, the butcher's daughter stood behind the counter with meat behind her on the hooks. Then a pig-sticker moved to town. He was young and strong and soon the townspeople were bringing him their pigs to stick and cut into good pieces of meat. The townspeople still came to the butcher shop for the heads and livers and hearts and tongues and skirts of cattle and sheep, but they bought their bacon from the pig-sticker. One day, a woman fed a calf's liver from the butcher shop to her young son and he died. The woman came into the butcher shop and slapped and scratched the face of the butcher's daughter. The butcher's daughter walked around the counter. She pushed the woman backwards so hard that the woman fell through the butcher shop window and the glass went into the woman's body and deep into the kidneys and the rump of the woman and she bled in a great spout and quickly the blood thickened and turned very black and the woman died. The butcher was cutting meat in the back of the shop. He did not come to the front of the shop. He did want anyone to connect his face with the dead woman who had fallen through the window in the front of the shop. He cut meat in the back of the shop and the butcher's daughter covered the woman with her apron in the front of the shop until the woman's people came and took the woman away. In the evening, the butcher asked his daughter to go away. The butcher loved his daughter. She was a very black, very merry girl and the butcher had no one else to stand in the front of the shop, but the butcher had decided that she had to go away. The butcher's daughter left the shop merrily. The butcher's daughter thought she might marry the pig-sticker, who was young and strong and did a good business and would soon have a shop of his own, but the pig-sticker had decided to marry the steel-grinder's daughter. Everywhere the butcher's daughter went, the townspeople recognized her from the butcher shop and they closed their doors to her. Men pelted her with old black-spotted meat. A washerwoman said she would hire the butcher's daughter. Instead of a bar of soap, the washerwoman gave the butcher's daughter a sponge of old meat. The butcher's daughter squeezed the sponge of old meat and the pink water ran down her wrist and stained her sleeve. The butcher's daughter became thin and her eyes grew a crust and she was grayer and grayer and less merry and black. Men no longer recognized the butcher's daughter except that the butcher's daughter had blood on her sleeve and the butcher's daughter had a very wide, very big, very dark mouth in which the teeth also darkened. The butcher's daughter could not chew the scraps of meat and the husks of old bread that the men threw to hit against her head and her back when she walked through the town. Rather, she sucked a rag that she dipped in what their wives left uncovered.

19

I gather the crumpled pages from the corner. I put them in the fireplace. The map is stuck to the wall where the food has wetted it. I scrape the map. I peel the map from the wall and put it in the fireplace. There is nothing to make the papers in the fireplace burn. There is no flint and steel. There is no phosphor. It is cold and dim in the nursery. I am tired. I lie down on the carpet in front of the fireplace. Spot lies down. Tamworth lies down. This is where they sleep in the nursery, on the carpet in the nursery. I like to the lie down on the carpet. There is no carpet in the field. I lay in the field. I stood up. I fell down. I lay in the field, the field the farmer chopped from the forest. I lay in the field. I cut a lump on my foot and a worm came out. It was a very black worm. The jackdaws circled me. They pecked my hands, my feet. A fat girl from the dairy passed by me. Good morning Mister Magpie, she said and I tried to strike her with a rock. There were no rocks in the field. There were furrows. I pushed my hands deep in a furrow, but there were no rocks. I threw clods at the milk pail. The clods came apart in the air. Mister Magpie, the fat girl said, but they were jackdaws. The fat girl swung her pail back and forth so that her fat wrist creased. She did not know jackdaws from magpies. I laughed on my back in the furrows, looking up. The fat girl's head was beside the blue sky and she did not know anything at all. In the dairy, Mister Cow, said the fat girl, but it was a wolfhound. I laughed at the fat girl, her fat bottom on the stool and her fat wrists creasing as she tugged at the udders of the wolfhound. The clod did not reach the pail. The clods came apart and the dirt fell onto my face. I wanted to strike the fat girl with a rock. Why weren't there rocks? In the ground, there are rocks. Someone had cleaned the rocks from the furrows, had dragged the rocks away in the sledge. It could not have been the farmer, the man who owned the field and the dairy and two daughters with hats. The farmer did not drag a sledge through the furrows, picking rocks. He rode on a horse, his short legs flapping on the sides of the horse, his short arms flapping the reins on the neck of the horse. Perhaps it was the fat girl from the dairy. She came in the night to the field and filled her pail with rocks so I could not strike her with rocks in the day. But in the ground, the rocks are always rising. The rocks rise up from deep in the ground so that when you pick the rocks from the furrows soon there are more rocks, many more rocks, rocks that float to the top of the field. The fat girl could not have taken away all of the rocks in the night. The rocks would come back. She would need to keep picking rocks, walking the furrows, picking rocks, and then when would she milk in the dairy? The farmer's two daughters are great big girls. They must drink great quantities of milk. They must treat their skin with milk below the hats. I have seen the two daughters dipping ladles in stone jugs of milk. At the top of the milk is the cream. The cream rises to the top of the milk and the two daughters drink the cream, great clots of cream. They don't know if the cream is from a cow or a wolfhound. I laughed again in the furrows. I dug harder for rocks and found only clods. I threw clods at the pail. Finally the fat girl was struck by clod. The clod broke apart on her teeth through the open lips as the fat girl said, Mister Magpie, Mister Magpie, and the jackdaws circled all around her. The fat girl dropped her pail and it tilted over in a furrow and loose dirt tumbled from the pail. There was no milk in the pail. There was dirt in the pail. What did the fat girl milk that she should have only dirt in her pail? The fat girl was crying and stumbling. What do you milk? I said to the fat girl. What do you milk in the night? The fat girl was crying. She milked the grave of the farmer's wife. That is what she milked. The farmer pressed her to the ground and her fat wrists creased up and down and the dirt went between her teeth. That is what the fat girl did in the night. Then who picked the rocks? I picked the rocks. That is why the farmer allowed me to sleep in the field, to sleep in the field all day with the rocks rising beneath me while I slept.

20

Get up, I say. Get up. Open your books. We will study rocks. The children do not move. I move. I pace. The children do not move. I rub my wrists together. I rub my wrists on the back of my neck. The nursery is damp. The walls are made of stone. The stone drips. Along the tops of the walls, women's faces. The faces are gray. They are gray masks of faces, gray masks in the masonry along the tops of the walls. The mouths are open like the mouth of the fireplace. We will study rocks, I say. Geology, says Spot. We study Geology. Tamworth says a word. I do not look at her. Her dress does not cover her thighs. The seams have ripped below her arms and the flesh of her breasts presses through the gaps. Tamworth says the word. She says the word. She says the word. Stop it, I say. Jasper, says Tamworth. Jasper. Jasper. Jasper, said the knife. Jasper. I scraped the bristles off the pigs. I was wet. I breathed hard. The steam burned my hands. The hot water ran over the skins of the pigs, loosening the bristles. I scraped deep. I scraped beneath the bristles and the skin came up in peels. There was no blood. The blood had drained through the necks. The blood had soaked into the straw. The blood had flowed into the road. The blood had filled the ditches in the road. First, the pole-ax through the skulls. Then the slits in the necks. Then the blood in the straw. Then the blood in the road. I scalded the pigs. I heaved the kettles. My hands burned. I used the knife. I used the candlestick. The knife said, jasper. The candlestick said, jasper. I breathed hard. White hairs clung to my arms, my skirt. I itched. The breath came hard through my teeth. It said, jasper. Jasper. The water was cooking the flesh beneath the skins. I was hungry. The flesh beneath the skins was almost cooked. The bristles were loosening. The skin was loosening. I could smell the hard flesh of the pig beneath the skin. The smell was thick and hot. I vomited into the straw and the dirty white mush lay on top of the blood. I lay down in the straw. It was wet. I heard screaming. The pigs were dead, but I heard screaming. The screaming was loud. I kicked the pigs. The pigs were hard. They were heavy and still. Each kick pushed my body backwards through the straw. My spine scraped through the straw. I kicked again and again. I pushed against the pigs with my heels but the pigs did not move. I slid through the straw. My skin came up in peels. The back of my head rubbed the straw, the dirt beneath the straw. Hot water was pouring on my breasts. I screamed. I could see the man who poured the water through the steam. I tried to crawl through the straw. I tried to hide between the bodies of the pigs, wedged between the pigs, my face pressed to the faces of the pigs. The nooses lashed around the snouts of the pigs burned my cheeks. I put my hands on my cheeks and my knuckles touched the teeth of the pigs through their lips.

21

The lesson is spoiled. I say, the lesson is spoiled. There will be no more lesson. We will sit on the carpet. Don't move, I say. Don't move. You are a rock. We are rocks in the nursery. We are clods of dirt in the nursery. This is the new lesson, I say. We are very still. We are quiet and still. Yes, says Tamworth. She wiggles. She plays with the threads on Spot's mouth. They are white threads. They stretch from the skin in the corners of his lips. They stretch thin between Tamworth's fingers and the lips. Tamworth rolls a white thread into a ball between her fingers. Spot picks at a piece of skin in the middle of his lip. He picks at a thread in the corner of his lips. He looks at Tamworth's fingers, the motions of her fingers as she rolls the thread. Tamworth is very close to Spot on the carpet. I am very close to Spot on the carpet. We are still, I say. We are quiet and still. Spot breathes out. It is wet. The wet breath wiggles the skin, the threads on his lips. I look at Spot's lips. I hold my hand in front of Spot's lips to feel the thickness of the breath. I don't touch the lips. I hold my hand close. The wet is very thick. It is a clod. Spot pushes the clod from his mouth. He pushes the clod from his mouth. His shoulders go up and down. We are still. Tamworth puts her head on her knees. She is still. She turns her head to the side. Her nostril pulls wide. A squealing noise is coming from the crib. Give it ragbaby, says Tamworth. Ragbaby, says Spot. Ragbaby. You are rocks, I say. Rocks on the carpet. We are heavy and still. We can be hit with a stick. We can be hit with a knife. We do not move. Tamworth's knees are white and round. Her face is white and wet. Her cheek is flat on her knees. Tamworth moves her dull eyes back and forth. I see Spot's fingers dart out fast and twist the flap that hangs from Tamworth's arm. Tamworth makes a sound. Wetness runs from the flattened mouth. The squealing noise is louder. In a grand house, there are rocks on the carpet. There is offal on the staircase. There are hams in the chimney. There are pigs in the crib. I want a hot slice of ham. I am very hungry. The cook must come to the nursery. She must come up the staircase. Do you hear cook? I say. Do you hear cook? In the hall, I hear blows. I hear cries. It is the Master. I will go to him. I will not. He will notice my dark hair, my long face. The dress hangs on me. The loose threads hold the dirt. I shake my dress. I scatter my dirt on the carpet. The carpet is a field. The Master is an old man. When he was young, he was a farmer. He farmed a field. He rode a horse. He had short, fat arms. No, the Master is not a farmer. He gets his milk from the farmer. He gets white milk from the farmer. The girls bring the milk from the dairy. The milk is brown. The milk has turned. The girls walk on the road with the milk. They lie down in the ditches. Flies settle on the milk while the girls lie in the ditches. They are rocks in the ditches. The sun is hot on the milk. The men block the sun for the girls. They block the sun. The girls fill their mouths to keep out the men. They put dirt in their mouths. They are rocks. They are clods. They gag. They spit dirt in the milk. The men cast shade in the ditches. The Master waits for the milk. The cook waits for the milk. The children wait for the cook. They wait for the lesson to end. They are little lambs. They are little ducks. They are little pigs. Dear little pigs. No, they are not pigs. The Mistress did not call them pigs. They are pups. She called them pups. Her own darling pups. In the nursery, I must finish the lesson. Spot pushes with his breath. He pushes. I am wet. I shut my eyes. Spot lies across me. Tamworth lies across me. I feel the hard tips of their fingers through my dress, pulling the buttons on my dress. I wiggle. We must be still. Spot and Tamworth must be still. They lie across me. My teats are wet. My tongue is short and wet. I lap the pups. My tongue is short and wet. I move my wet mouth rapidly against the pups, the wiggling limbs and necks of the pups. My teats give milk. They give no milk. The milk comes from the dairy. The children drink milk. They eat cakes. The governess watches them eat. Her skin shines with grease. Her hair shines with grease. Her skin has spots. She plays with her spots while they eat.

22

The vicar had a daughter. The vicar's daughter sang behind a hedge. The vicar's daughter sang like a linnet. She took a large book behind the hedge. She took a cup of overdrawn tea. Hours are always passing. The books are bound in buckram. The little book is mensuration. The large book, voyages and lives. The vicar's daughter sang. The poplars swayed. The vicar was afloat in the mill pond. His clothes were folded on a stone. The tea grew very dark and cold. The vicar's daughter climbed into the gig. Linnets sang along the roadway. Beside the manse, the children played with sticks and cords. They tipped her trunk. They dragged her dresses through the mud. They struck her face with clods. Hours are always passing. The large girl is Mistress Ann. The little boy is Master Charles. The vicar's daughter crawled into the fire. She held a little, singeing book. She chased the children through the mole traps in the garden. She ran behind the peat house. She followed sounds into the stables. The vicar's daughter climbed upon a three-legged stool. She cut the dog down from the beam. The dog sagged. The rope thudded on the straw. Weasels were nailed to the fence posts. The mole traps swarmed with flies. Down the wooded bank, primroses peeked from twisted roots. The vicar's daughter sang. She sat in the brook. The boy stopped kicking beneath her. The water felt good. The vicar's daughter let the water numb her hands.

23

Tamworth wiggles in her chair. She makes fists of her fat little hands. Ragbaby, says Tamworth. It wants ragbaby. She puts the fists to her ears. The squealing noise does not stop. Tamworth wiggles. The reddish lids twitch against the bulge of her eyes. Tamworth is grown. She makes a smell that comes from her lap in the chair. Her dress is bunched in her lap in the chair. The fabric is gray. It smells. She puts her fat little hands in her lap. She wiggles. I hear the air move in her mouth, through her lips. She is grown. Tamworth shifts in the nursery chair. Her thighs hang over the sides of the chair. She needs a new dress, a big dress, for the ball. There is a ballroom in the house. The house is grand. There are towers and there must be a ballroom. There is a music Master. He crossed the moat. He wore gloves. His coat split in the back like a bird's tail or the hoof of a pig. He had a fine high voice and he sang as he crossed the moat. He whistled as he crossed the moat. Tamworth must learn to play music. A lady plays music. A lady goes to a room. Not the nursery. A lady does not suffer the mess of the nursery, the smell of the nursery. A lady goes to a drawing room. It is called a drawing room. Beneath the ballroom of a grand house, there is a drawing room. There is a drawing Master. He carried paints across the moat. He dropped the paints into the moat and the paints lay on top of the water. Yellow lay on top of the water. Red lay on top of the water. Flies settled on the red. The drawing Master made paint with urine from the dairy. The cows lifted their tails and let out their urine and the drawing Master crouched beneath with a bucket. He carried a bucket across the field. The bucket billowed in the cold. In a cup, a clod. In a cup, a pour of blood. Red flies followed the drawing Master into the house. A lady sits at an easel. She licks the tip of a brush, the fine white hairs of the brush. She dips the brush in a paint. No, a lady does not. She does not dip. She strokes. She strokes a string. She strokes a string with the tips of her fingers. Her guests cannot hear her brats when they squeal in the nursery. The string makes a fine high sound. The drawing room is delighting to guests. It is filled with fine high sounds. There is no smell. There is a smell, but guests do not notice a smell. A lady does not notice smells. Tamworth must not study smells. Tamworth must study the different sounds of the strings. That is how a lady does not notice the squealing. When the wind comes from the dairy, from the fields of the farmer, from the lanes of the town, the open ditches of the town, the coal bins of the town, the earth closets of the town, when the wind comes down the staircase, across the mess on the staircase, from the nursery, from the crib in the nursery, there is a smell, but a lady does not say, There is a smell. A lady sings between her lips, which are open only slightly. She does not say, There is pus in the milk. There is ocher and water in the milk. There is piss in the paint. There is a bucket of piss behind the curtains. There is a drawing Master with my daughter. They are behind the curtains. There is squealing. They are squealing in the curtains. The guests are in the drawing room. They cannot see behind the curtains. Only from the orchard could they see behind the curtains, through the glass to the backside of the curtains. A lady pours the milk from the pitcher in the tea. I have failed in my lessons to Tamworth. Smells and rocks are not for a lady. Squeals are not for a lady. Tamworth must listen to the sound of strings. She must put her ear to the hole in my foot. She puts her ear to the hole in my ear and listens for the chiming, the pealing, the thin sound of metal striking metal in the hole.

24

I walk to the crib and touch the iron rails with my fingers. I look down at the crib, at the rags in the crib. The rags are piled very high. The squealing is very loud. I put my hand in the crib. I apply pressure to the rags. The rags compress. The rags compress. They are cold and damp. Nothing moves in the rags. Nothing moves. There is squealing. Give it ragbaby, says Tamworth. She gets out of her chair and crawls on the carpet. Her skirt does not cover her thighs. Spot crawls after Tamworth on the carpet. He pulls Tamworth's skirt. Ragbaby, says Spot, Ragbaby, but it is Tamworth's skirt, the folds of her skirt. I take the knife from the tray and stroke the rails of the crib with the knife, so that they make a high, fine sound, and I sing a note that is louder than the squealing, a high fine note. Make this note, I say to Tamworth. She struggles with Spot on the carpet. He has taken off his shirt to truss her hands. He trusses so her hands are palm to palm, and she slips her hands free. She shrieks. She hits with her hands. She kicks a leg of the rocking horse. She kicks a leg of the table. Spot laughs. His cheek spiders with cracked veins from the hit. He kneels on her thighs. Spot does not know how to truss. He does not know knots. He must study knots. Boys must learn knots. The nursery is damp and the smell is stronger. I drop the knife in the crib. I back away from the crib. I feel Tamworth's damp hand close around my ankle. I look down at her face. Her hair has come loose from her braids. The colorless hairs stick to the wet skin of her face, the pink veins that raise the skin of her face. The walls of the nursery come closer. They come closer. The nursery is damp and cold. A nursery is a crib with high walls and a lid. It is a crib of damp stone. I crouch. I cover my face with my arms. I am pushed against Tamworth and Spot. I am pushed against Tamworth and Spot by the walls of the nursery. They breathe hard. They move beneath me.

25

The tray is empty. The pitcher is empty. Flakes fall from the corners of Spot's mouth. White flakes fall. Tamworth rubs deposits from her teeth with the hem of her dress. The deposits are white. That is where the milk has gone. It has dried on Tamworth's teeth. It has dried in the corners of Spot's mouth. Children need milk. Children need milk to grow. On the carpet, there is narrow-necked bottle. It has a rubber nipple. It has a pigskin tube. I pick up the bottle. It has deposits in its narrow neck. The rubber nipple is cracked and hard. It is clogged with deposits. It smells. There is no milk in the bottle. Where is the milk? I ask. Where is the milk? There must be milk in the kitchen. There is milk in the moat. From the high window, I see milk in the moat. The moat is gray with the milk. The cook throws bad milk in the moat. She throws brown apples. She throws white scraps, the white scraps the Master cuts from the meat. The white things that crawl from the meat. The green slime that she carves from the meat. The blisters of meat. I see the blisters of meat on the moat. There are white flies on the blisters. There are black flies on the blisters. The moat is buzzing with flies. Things have died below the flies on the moat. They bump the flies from the below. The flies ripple up and down on the moat, the skin of flies on the moat. I could walk across the moat, on the thick skin of the moat. I could walk to the orchard. In the orchard, the Master lifted her dress. He pulled the skirt over her head, he covered her head. He covered the mess of her head. Her long pale hairs had blackened with fluids. He hid her hairs with the dress. He hid her face with the dress. He stroked her face through the thin cloth of the dress. Above, he stroked. Below, he jerked. The Master's dogs came around. The Master's dogs came around the Master. The Master jerked. The Master put his knees on the apples. He had a stick. He hit the dogs with his stick. The dogs whined. They climbed on the Master. They pressed against the Master. They pressed the Master in the apples. The dogs jerked against the Master. They jerked against the jerking back and legs of the Master. He swung his stick. He hit the dogs. They whined. The Master whined. Poor little dogs. The Master rolled over. He held the dogs. He held the dogs with his knees, with his elbows and knees. With his hands, he pulled the ears of his dogs. He stroked the heads of the dogs. Poor little dogs. They dripped blood from their mouths. They put their mouths on the Master's neck, on the Master's mouth. The Master opened his mouth. The dogs put their mouths on his mouth. They put their mouths on his chin and his mouth. The Master's mouth dripped with the blood from the dogs. She wiggled out of her dress. She uncovered her hair, her face. She crawled through the apples. She tried to climb the black boughs of the tree. She dragged a rope. The Master knelt beneath the tree. She stood on his shoulder. She hooked her leg around the branch.

The Master pushed her fat bottom. She clung to the branch. I pushed her fat bottom. She dragged a rope. I gave her the farmer's rope. She knotted the rope on the bough. She swung down. She dangled.

26

The woodcutter had a daughter. The woodcutter's daughter was big like the woodcutter. Her arms were big. Her legs were big. Everyone said what a big girl the woodcutter's daughter, a very big girl. If only the woodcutter's daughter were a son, the son would go into the forest with his father. He would help his father cut the wood. The woodcutter's daughter did not go to the forest. She went to the town. She did the washing in town while the woodcutter cut wood in the forest. The woodcutter's daughter sat on a stool and did the washing. Water ran down the legs of the stool. The woodcutter's daughter wore a dress. The dress became dark. The woodcutter's daughter lifted her hands from the tub. Water ran down her arms. Water ran down her legs. Water ran down the legs of the stool. Water pooled around the tub. The woodcutter's daughter bent over on the stool. She gave birth to a son. The son was big. He lay in the tub with the washing and the crown of his head touched one side of the tub and the heels of his feet touched the other. He was a big son. The woodcutter's daughter took the son home, but the woodcutter did not come home. He did not come home from the forest. The woodcutter's daughter went into the forest. She found an ax in a stump. The metal of the ax was dark and there were hairs on the metal, white hairs that were the length of a man's hairs or the hairs on an animal. The woodcutter's daughter pulled the ax from the stump. She used the blade of the ax to cut the hairs on her head. She held the ax steady and rubbed her hairs back and forth on the blade until the hairs broke. The blade cut into the back of her head as she cut the hairs that grew in the back of her head. Blood ran down her neck. Blood ran down her shoulders. Blood ran down from her neck and across both her shoulders. Her dress became dark. She took off her dress. She put her dress on the stump. She took a shirt from a dark bush with red thorns. The red thorns had pulled white threads from the shirt. Beneath the brown leaves on the path, she saw trousers the color of leaves. She put on the trousers. She walked through the forest. She entered a town. The town had a baker. It had a butcher. It had a farmer. It had a man who boiled bones and a man who sold worsted cloth from a wagon and a man who removed what thickened beneath the tongues of chickens and horses. It had a blacksmith and a vicar and a rich man who owned a mill on the water, but the town did not have a woodcutter. The people of the town smiled when the woodcutter's daughter took the dark ax down from her shoulder.

27

The orchard is altogether changed. Where are the apples, the soft, rotten apples? The orchard is not brown. It is hard and gray. The walls are hard and gray. They drip. They are stone. The trees are stone. The trees have grown together. The faces in the knots of the trees are gray. Every face has an open mouth. The mouths are filled with fluid. The fluid drips down the walls. The pigs press around. They dig in the orchard. They grunt. They squeal. They move against me. They push with wet faces, hard, wet faces. The teeth are inside the faces, behind the thick skin of the faces. They have white hairs on their faces. White hairs cluster around their eyes. They press against me. They dirty the dress. They smear dung on the dress. I can't breathe with them against me. I can't breathe. They are squealing. It is coming from the crib. It is coming from the carpet. The pigs are digging through the carpet. There is earth beneath the carpet. The pigs put their noses in the earth. They open their mouths. They eat the earth. They eat the tubers in the earth, the white roots in the earth, the tapered root that comes from the earth. They dig deeper than the dogs. They dig a deep hole in the nursery. I wait for her to come into the nursery, to hook her fingers on the edge of the hole and climb up into the nursery. I would sever her neck with the housekeeper's shovel but I have only the covers of books.

28

You can see into the orchard from the tower. You can see into the orchard from the forest. On one side of the orchard, tower. On the other side, forest. I saw through the bushes in the forest, lights in the tower, shapes in the orchard. The house lit the orchard. It made shadows in the orchard. I sat in the bushes. She held the bough of the tree with her hands and her knees. She clung to the bough. She kicked her feet. She swung down. She dangled. Her face was red and wet. The spots on her face were red and wet. She lifted her knees as she dangled then she let her knees drop. She dropped to the earth. She lay in the apples. The Master lay in the apples. He pulled himself through the apples with his elbows. He slid through the apples. She pulled herself with her heels through the apples. She slid beneath the Master. He jerked against her. He jerked against her. He lifted her shoulders and her head fell back. The hairs on her head hung down to the apples. The crown of her head hung down to the apples. Her head hit the apples. She jerked up and down. Her head hit the apples. The brown skins of the apples clung to her neck. They clung to her shoulders. She slid. The Master pushed on his belly through the apples. Her back slid through the apples. The Master lifted his hand. He hit her head with an apple. He hit her head with a rock. The rock was brown like the apples. It was long and brown. It was a stick. The Master hit her head with a stick. He beat her head with a stick. He jerked against her. He beat with a stick. Black fluid darkened her head, it darkened her hair. Her body dripped with rain. Her body dried in the sun. She thinned in the sun. She withered.

29

Put fat on the opening. Rub the fat with your hand. Rub the fat
hard with your hand, with the palm of your hand. Slip inside.
Slip the boot hook inside. Pull from inside the opening. That
is how things are born, even in a grand house. With fat and an
opening. With a hand or a hook. The children listen. They have
knocked over the chairs. They have knocked over the rocking
horse. Tamworth leans on the neck of the horse on the carpet.
The wooden runners of the horse press into her thighs. She is
very fat. She is fat and round. Her breasts are fat and round.
They strain the seams of her gray dress. No one has taught
them about the fat and the hook. In a grand house, the Mistress births hard. She dies. She dies with blood in the bed. The
pigs do not die. The cows do not die. The Mistress dies. In a
grand house, she dies. I rubbed the fat with my hand. I dug
through the dried deposits with my hand. I dug fast. I pushed
with my hand. I pushed in the hook. I hooked. I pulled hard.

The hot air filled my mouth. I gagged. I pulled. The sweat ran down my arms and ran down the handle of the hook. The opening spilled. It opened farther and spilled. Brown dung spilled in the fluid. My feet slid. I braced against heaving. I was pressed against the wall. My wrist cracked. I screamed. I could not pull with the hand. I took the other hand and I pulled. My shoulder made a sound. My shoulder cracked. I pulled harder. I slid and the weight of my body pulled down. It pulled down. It pulled down. I lay down flat on the dung. I lay down flat on the fluid. My neck itched with straw. My arms burned. My shoulder burned. The opening spilled and I brought it toward me. It moved toward me. I felt the blows, the hard blows, in my stomach and thighs and it moved against me, wet and hard. The deposits and dung went thick in my mouth so I was very quiet. I did not scream. My mouth leaked. It bubbled. I did not scream. Tamworth listens to the lesson. Her mouth is open. Her mouth is dry. It does not leak. She licks her teeth to moisten the deposits. She wiggles. She is ready for a lesson. There is no hook in the nursery. The hooks are in the kitchen. Meat hangs on the hooks. I will take the meat from the hooks. I will carry the meat to the moat. I will put the green meat on the moat. The meat will not sink. The moat is thick. There is a thick skin on the moat. It ripples. Beneath the meat, curds. Beneath the meat, scraps. Black flies cover the meat. White flies cover the meat. They take the shape of the meat. Little wings on the meat. Sacks bump the meat from the below. Spot fills the sacks. I have seen him fill sacks. He drops sacks in the moat. Things move in the sacks. No, I will not go to the moat. I will not put meat in the moat. Meat should hang. In the kitchen, it dangles. It grows scabs. It grows wings. I will cut the meat from the hooks. I will tie the meat to the beam. It will dangle. I will take the old fat from the can. I will take the old fat. I will take honey. I will take hooks. I will bring the hooks to the nursery.

The children have only learned one lesson. Who taught them the lesson? She did not teach them. She taught them globes. She taught them geology. They wrote names in the book. They wrote figures in the book. They counted dogs. Many dogs fit in a sack. Many small dogs. There are many steps to the kitchen. There are many steps to the tower. From the tower, the dogs look small. The Master looks small. They watch the small Master. He carries a sack. No, he carries a dress, a shape in a dress. His head is an apple. It is the size of an apple. Tamworth puts her face on the glass. She flattens her face. She pushes. Spot pushes. He puts his hands on the glass. Tamworth flattens her face on the glass. Spot pushes. Fine white hairs cluster on his cheeks, Tamworth's white hairs, long white hairs. They come loose from her head. They stick to Spot's cheeks. He pushes. Her reddish eyelids twitch on the glass. He pushes. He counts hairs. Tamworth bangs on the glass. Her wet mouth makes an O on the glass. It makes a square on the glass. He pushes hard. She says, Master. She says, Master. He is too small to be seen.

30

The nursery door is open. It is a wooden door, a small wooden door; a child could push open the door. Where are the children? It is a dark time of day. Not night. No, it is a dark time of year. It is a dark season. The walls are very gray. The carpet is wet. The chairs are empty. Where are the children? The nursery is small. The nursery is meant for children, small children. There must be children somewhere in the nursery. Children laugh and play in the nursery. They play tricks. They tip the rocking horse. They tip the two chairs. They whistle to the dogs that go up and down the staircase. They kiss the dogs. They hit the dogs. They climb into the desks. They climb into the crib. They make holes in the carpet. They crawl into the holes. They wiggle. They laugh. They are rosy and dear. Little dears, that is what she called them. She counted to three. She put her hands on her eyes. She stood by the crib. She covered her eyes with a rag. She counted to ten. Charles has 10 apples.

He gives his sister 7. How many has he left? He spends 6 cents for apples. 9 cents for cakes. A cake is worth 3 apples. How hungry is Charles? Twice he drinks 2 quarts of milk. 2 children start from the same place. They travel in the same direction. How many halves in 3 apples? On the wagon: 1 sack of apples. On the wagon: 1 sack of sugar. 1 pail of milk. 2 barrels of pork. Charles wishes to divide his books into piles. 3 piles. 10 books. How many books in each pile? How many dogs in each sack? A drover gave 7 sheep to the farmer. He got a cow and a calf. A book for 10 cents and a top for 7. Charles ate 5 apples as often as his sister ate cakes. Ann ate cakes. How many cakes? The man had 5 sacks. He had twice as many daughters as sacks. Not sacks. The remainder between apples and cakes. What is the remainder? The unit is cakes. How many cakes? His daughters are how many cakes? Where are the sacks? A tree has 10 branches. 2 apples hang from a branch. 1 apple kicks. 1 apple has spots. It swings. It dangles. She counted to ten. She counted ten apples. Ten little pigs eat ten little apples. The pigs are still hungry. Ten brown soft apples. Ten white hard pigs. Pigs are not little. They are hungry. They dig ten little holes. She felt with her hands on the carpet. Hairs stuck to her hands. Crumbs stuck to her hands. She felt the edge of the tray. She felt the belly of a dog, the thick hair, the stiff, cold belly of a dog. She felt the stiff leg of a dog. The little dears—where could they be? They'd left behind their crumbs. They'd left behind their dogs. The nursery door banged on its hinges. The windows were open. There was a draft in the nursery. It was a dark time of day. Through the rag, it was night. It was wet. She banged her hip on the crib. She banged her shin on the table. She felt the rails of the crib with her hands. Little dears. She felt the frame of the door. She felt the cold in the hall. She felt the first step with her toe. She felt the second step with her toe. She felt the second step with her heel. She felt the third with her heel. She felt the fifth with her knee. She felt the sixth with her wrist. She felt the seventh with her chin, the eighth with her chin, the ninth with her chin, the tenth with her wrist, her ankle, her hip, her neck, her nose, her palm, her shin, her spine, her rib, her chin, her chin, her chin, her chin.

31

The farmer had two daughters, each daughter like the other. They rode on dainty ponies, each pony like the other. Sometimes they walked. Arm in arm, they walked from the farmhouse to the fields. They sat on a low stone wall. They clapped hands. They walked into the forest. They found the hovel of the half-wit. He worked for the farmer. He dunged the fields for the farmer. He dunged the fruit trees for the farmer. He drove a cart of dung. The daughters did not see the cart and so they approached the hovel. The trees had dropped their acorns. The daughters approached the hovel over acorns. They felt the pressures of the acorns through the soles of their shoes. The hovel had a door, a plank for a door. It hung open on a broken hinge. The daughters went through the door. They felt smooth dirt—cold smooth dirt—through the soles of their shoes. They had expected the hovel to smell like dung, but the smell in the hovel was a different smell. The daughters breathed hard through their mouths. They looked straight ahead. They turned their faces to the side and vomited, each in her own corner of the room. Straight ahead of the daughters lay the half-wit. The daughters looked straight ahead. They had never seen a naked man and now they saw the half-wit. The half-wit's legs were thin and bent, but his chest was very wide and the stomach pushed up very high. He had white hairs growing on the tops of his shoulders and around his nipples. Something had bitten at the face of the half-wit, at the soft nose and lips of the half-wit, and at the groin of the half-wit. The daughters could see white through the torn cheek of the half-wit, the white of the half-wit's teeth. The dainty ponies of the daughters had things that came down from their bellies when they made their thick streams. Across the white thin leg of the half-wit, the half-wit's thing looked black. The biting had made his thing black with blood and swollen so that it cracked on the sides and the knob. Yellow-clear fluid leaked from the sides and the knob and wetted the half-wit's leg. Arm in arm, the daughters walked to the half-wit. They could not walk around the half-wit. The hovel was too small. The head of the half-wit touched the back wall of the hovel. One of the daughters touched the half-wit's thing with the toe of her shoe. She felt nothing through the toe of her shoe. The knob on the thing was as large as an apple. Touching the knob on the thing with the toe of her shoe, the daughter's face did not look different from the face of the daughter who did not touch, who stood with her shoes on the dirt.

32

The knob had a daughter. She was a fluid. No, she was a worm.
She was not a worm. She was a thread. She was a hair. The dog
had a hair. The pig had a hair. The milk had a hair. Look in the
milk. There is a hair. It is thicker at the root. It is long and thin.
It is sticky at the root. It smells. The dung had a daughter. She
was a smell. She was a wet smell. She stuck to the foot. She stuck
to the stairs. She said, listen, but she was a smell. Do you hear a
smell? said the cook. Do you hear a smell? said the gardener. We
cannot hear a smell. You cannot hear a smell. The housekeeper
wiped the smell with a rag. The rag had a daughter. She squealed.
There are eggs in the rags, said the cook. There are worms in the
rags. There are flies in the rags. She put the meat in the rags. She
put the rags in the sack. She put the sack in the hole. The hole
had a daughter. She was a rock. No, she was a clod. She was a fat,
wet clod. The farmer made his stream on the clod. The Master
stirred the stream and the clod. He made mud with his stick.

33

The nursery is changed. The sounds have changed. It is not squealing. It is not banging. It is dripping. The nursery drips. The chimney drips. On the roof of a grand house, chimneys, a forest of chimneys, thin chimneys, black chimneys. The Master walks in the forest of chimneys. The forest is not safe. It is slick. It is steeply pitched. Dogs run after the Master, slide after the Master. Their nails scratch on the slates. The Master walks from gable to gable. He rests by a chimney. He leans. He puts his hands on the hairs where they thicken. He jerks against a chimney, the black slot at the top of the chimney. His white hairs have changed. They are black. Between his legs, black soot, the black heads of the dogs, the flapping ears of the dogs, the red tongues of the dogs. Above the nursery, the attic. Above the attic, slates, gray slates, black chimneys, the Master. On top he is white. Below, black. He jerks with his stick. He is above the nursery. He drips. I crawl to the mouth of the fireplace. The stone is cold. The ashes are wet. I put my hands in the ashes, my knees in the ashes. I put my head in the chimney. The air comes apart in my mouth. I gag. My eyes burn. I press my face to the stone of the chimney. Fluids run on the stone. I lay on a low stone wall. It was hot. There was a sound. I crawled on the stone. I tried to crawl on the stone to the shade. Hairs stuck to my hands. I crawled through the hairs. The shade was far away in the forest. All around: the field. The yellow field. The field made a sound. The sound itched. I couldn't hear it. It itched. My eyes burned. I let my head hang. My tongue came out of my mouth to wet the corners of my lips. I crawled. I touched a shape on the stone. The hairs thickened. They made a shape. I touched the shape. It was a cat. I saw the face of a cat, the open eyes of the cat. I looked through the eyes of the cat to the stone. I put my fingers beneath the cat and I lifted. It flipped. It was only the skin of the cat. Flipped, it was white. It was dry and white. I lifted the skin. It flew up the chimney like ash.

34

The nursery is filled with books. There are books on the carpet. There are books on the chairs. The crib is filled with books. The covers of the books are black. Each page is a cat, the skin of a cat. The children flip the cats. They rub the cats. They scrape the cats with their nails. The children are vastly changed. They are quiet. They are piles of black fabrics and cats. They are cats. They are little skinned cats. I open a book. I try to look through the book, the holes in the book. I open the holes with the knife. I see my foot. I look through the hole in my foot. A carpet is made of strings, black strings. The strings come up through the hole in my foot. Tamworth has a hole, says Spot. Tamworth has a hole in her foot. I laugh. Spot is quiet. He is a book. The children are books. They are quiet. I don't hear you, I say. It is quiet. I hear drips. Above, I hear bangs. I hear jerks. I hear scrapes. Don't move, I say. Don't move. You are a book. A book is filled with skin. Little skins.

You need to clean the hairs from the skins. You need to scrape the hairs from the skins. Spot is changed. He sits on the chair. No, he tips over the chair. He lies on the carpet. He takes down his trousers. He puts his hands on the hairs. He scrapes with his nails. He scrapes. He scrapes. Hairs fall on the carpet. Tamworth squirms. She has her hands in her thighs. She scrapes. She scrapes hard. She kicks the runners of the rocking horse. She kicks the belly. She kicks the neck. She pushes her body backwards. Her dress bunches. Her white thighs are very big. Her head touches the iron leg of the crib. Her white thighs are marked with fluids. They are shapes, red shapes. It is a map, a wet map. It is the field. It is the town. Where is the nursery? I say. I crawl close to the map. It smells. Little white hairs root in the shapes. At the roots, red. At the tips, white. The skin shakes. I put my mouth on the shapes. I smear the shapes with my mouth. They taste hot. They taste thick. Tamworth hits my nose with her wrist. She moves her wrist. Between her thighs, she scrapes. She scrapes. She makes a hole. A worm crawls out. I put the worm in the crib, in the rags in the crib. I look down at the crib. I look down at the children. I smile. I make the shape of the nursery with my mouth.

35

After the lesson, we will go to the forest. We will take the globe to the forest. We will take the books to the forest. We will ride the rocking horse all through the forest. We will push the horse with our legs. How many legs? I say. Six legs, says Spot. Six legs, says Tamworth. We have six legs. A fly, I say. We are a fly. A white fly. We live in a blister of meat. What is a house? I say. A blister of meat. There is no meat, I say. There is no house. We live in the forest. We live in the field. We pick stones from the field. We lie down in the furrows. We lie down. A fat girl passes. She is the cook. She has a tray of cakes. She has a pitcher of milk. She rests the tray on a clod, the pitcher on a clod. She sits on a clod. She scrapes her sores with a knife. She wipes her knife on the cakes. The gardener passes. He puts lilies in the milk. The stalks fill with milk. The throats fill with milk. They drip milk. The petals turn white. They drop on the clods. They are cream, great clots of cream. Ladies drink cream. They turn white. Their skin is clean and white. The farmer rides through the fields on a horse. He has two legs. They flap on the sides of the horse. He slides from the horse. He sits on a clod. He puts his thing in the milk. He drains his thing in the milk. He holds me close. What is that smell? says the farmer. A lady won't know. She won't know. She isn't taught smells. I don't know. What is a smell? I don't know. It is milk, I say. It is the lilies in milk. I laugh. Flies tickle my foot. They crawl from the hole in my foot. Each fly has six legs. Each leg has six hairs, little white hairs. I pull a hair from my foot. A long white hair. With a needle and a hair, I could stitch the hole. I could fasten the button to the hole. I could close the hole. I could cover the hole. Something fell from her mouth. Her foot slipped again and again. She dropped. She screamed. She jerked. Something fell from her mouth. It fell on the grass. It was small. What is small? I say. A child. An apple. A child is small. An apple is small. A key is small. A button is small. It was small like a button. I sat in the field. I found a button attached to a hair. I followed the hair to the house. The hair wound through the house. It wound through the hooks. It wound through the rails. It wound around the knob of her door. I touched the knob. I pushed the door open. Her neck was tied to the bed, to the tester of the bed. She dangled. Something small had fallen from her mouth. I climbed onto the bed. I put my hand in the dark between her breasts, in the hole between her breasts. I crawled into the hole.

36

I look at the crib. I look at the window. I look along the top of
the wall. I look at the faces, gray faces, gray masks of women's
faces. Every mouth is open. The Master watches. He watches
through the mouths in the masonry. I throw the tray at the
wall. I throw the pitcher at the wall. I hit the wall with the chair.
I breathe hard. I put the chair on the carpet. I sit on the chair.
I look down. I look at my foot. I hear a puff of air. It comes
from my foot, from the hole in my foot. There are no more
fluids in my foot. There is air. I am very slim. I am very light
and slim. I am very dry. I am filled with air. I hear the puff. It
does not come from my foot. It comes from above. It comes
through the mouth of the mask. The Master is speaking softly.
He whispers. He doesn't want her to hear. He doesn't want
them to hear. He is breathing a word. I don't know the word. I
can't hear the word. I stand. I can't hear the word. The Master
breathes the word through the wall, through the mask in the

wall. I open a book. I flip through the book. I put my fingers in the book. My mouth comes close to the book. Is this the word? I say. Is this the word? There is no one in the nursery. I breathe hard. I breathe louder than the Master. I can't hear him breathe. I can't hear him speak. I touch a page of the book. I put my eye on the page, the wet of my eye on the page. The eyelid twitches. It twitches on the page. My eye burns. It leaks fluid. Fluid runs on my face. It runs on the page. I put my mouth on the page. I flatten my mouth on the page. I flatten my nose on the page. I breathe hard. I suck the page. I pull the page between my lips. It pulls against my teeth, against my tongue. I wet the page. I smell the fluids on the page. I smell the page. It has a taste. It has a smell. The Master breathes a word. Is this the word? I can't hear him. The page comes apart in my mouth. I gag. Is this the word? Is this the word? Is this the word? Yes, it is the word. My mouth knows the word. It is the word that the Master intends for me. It is mine.

.

THE LEAST BLACKSMITH

1

My brother the blacksmith must hire a striker. My brother is a young man. Some day he may have a son. It is best for a blacksmith to have a son for a striker. When the blacksmith retires, the striker takes over the forge. The striker carries on the good name of the forge. His name is the same as his father's, and so his name is the same as the name of the forge.

My brother the blacksmith was our father's striker. Our father tapped with his hammer and my brother struck the iron. Our father was very happy with my brother. My brother never made mistakes. He always struck exactly where our father wanted. Our father said that he had been right to give my brother his name. He said that my brother would surpass him as blacksmith. Our father had plans to expand and modernize the forge. My brother would be the blacksmith in a large, modern forge. He could not help but surpass our father. Our father had surpassed his father and his father had not made a single improvement to the forge. Our father had done better work than his father with the same tools. My brother would do better work than our father with better tools. Our father did not make any improvements to the forge.

One moment our father was tapping the iron with his hammer, standing up, facing my brother across the anvil. He jerked the hand that held the hammer. He tapped his chest with the hammer. My brother struck our father's chest with the sledge. He struck exactly where our father had indicated. Our father's eyes closed. His mouth opened. He turned a quarter-turn. He fell across the hearth. My brother sent me to town to fetch the doctor. The doctor is a thin but purposeful man. He came with me right away. I was afraid that I was leading the doctor to the wrong place. The ground vibrates when you approach the forge. You can hear the clanging of hammer and sledge. The ground did not vibrate. I heard nothing. As the doctor and I came up the hill, I could see the forge. It looked like the forge, but it could not be the forge. That soundless building could not be the forge. The double doors of the forge stood open. There was our father on the floor of the forge. The doctor was surprised to see that our father's face was burned. He took our father's wrist between his fingers. He held our father's wrist. He laid our father's hand on his chest exactly where our father tapped with the hammer and my brother struck with the sledge. The doctor sat back on his heels. He lit a cigar. For a time the doctor did not say anything. My brother and I watched the doctor's lips pull at the cigar. There was no sound in the forge. The doctor smiled. The cigar did not fall because the doctor held the cigar with his teeth. He removed the cigar from his mouth and extinguished the coal with his fingers. He worked the end of the cigar through our father's fingers. Our father held the extinguished cigar on his chest.

The doctor stood and addressed my brother He said that he had been friends with our father when they were small boys. Our father and the doctor played mumblety-peg on the wharves. The doctor had smoked his first cigar with our father. The friendship did not end until they reached adulthood and quarreled over a woman. I never knew our father had been friends with a doctor. It must have been a wonderful friendship if the doctor remembered it so clearly. The doctor offered my brother a cigar. He did not offer me a cigar, although he admitted he had been very young when he first smoked a cigar with our father. Since becoming a doctor he could not offer a cigar to a child. He hoped I understood. My brother dropped his cigar on the floor where it was spoiled by the water he had poured from the tub. I had never seen my brother behave clumsily. He moved about the forge as though he did not know where he was. The doctor said he would take our father's body to his office. At his office, he would be able to reconstruct the last moments of our father's life using his new medical equipment. The doctor had traveled by ship to a conference where he received training on the equipment. The doctor was glad his first clinical trial would be with our father. The doctor said it felt right. My brother did not know how much to pay the doctor. He did not want to show his ignorance about something as important as doctor's fees. He gave the doctor a heavy bag of money, all the money our father had collected to deposit in the bank for the month. The doctor said our father would have been proud of my brother. Even though many years had passed since they played mumblety-peg on the wharves, the doctor still knew a thing or two about our father.

Our father was always proud of my brother. My brother developed quickly. Customers often mistook my brother for our father. Customers who came to the forge greeted my brother by our father's name. Our father's name is also my brother's name. My brother responded politely to the customers. He said that he was not the blacksmith. He was the blacksmith's striker. When the customers saw our father, they realized their mistake. They asked if my brother and our father were brothers. They could not believe that my brother was scarcely more than a child.

My brother did not expect to be blacksmith so soon. The first customers who came to the forge after our father died did not notice that our father was no longer the blacksmith. They saw my brother standing at the double doors of the forge. They were used to seeing two men at the double doors of the forge. They asked my brother what had happened to his striker. My brother said he needed to hire a striker. The customers suggested that he hire his son. My brother did not seem proud that I had been mistaken for his son. He did not respond to the customers.

2

The forge is on the hill. It has the highest elevation of any business in the town. Our house is behind the forge. Our house is smaller than the forge. There are two windows in the front of the house. You cannot see the bay from the windows. The windows look onto the back of the forge. There are boards nailed on either side of each window. It is as though the windows have shutters. The boards are not shutters. They have no hinges. Our mother nailed the boards alongside the windows for decoration. She liked decoration. I like decoration too. The boards alongside the windows are my favorite thing about the house. Our mother added decoration to the house, but she did not add decoration to the forge. The forge has not changed in any way since the time of our father's father. My brother tells me he will expand and modernize the forge. My brother is a wonderful blacksmith. As soon as he has a striker, he will expand and modernize the forge. I am my brother's only relative. It is best that I work as his striker.

My brother works all day and all night in the forge finishing the job our father could not finish. My brother's lips are dark. The skin beneath his eyes is dark. I sweep the floor and pump the bellows. I watch my brother work alone at the anvil. Sweat pours from my brother. He finishes our father's job. It is a feat to finish the job without our father, my brother alone, working all day and all night at the anvil. He will not be able to finish more jobs alone. The work is too hard without the help of a striker. My brother must hire a striker. It is best for a blacksmith to have a son for a striker. You do not have to pay a son wages. A son works to earn his name.

I want to work for my brother. He does not have to pay me wages. My brother and I live together in the house behind the forge. I do not know what I would do with wages. I could decorate the house with paper notes. The gray and pink paper notes are more appealing than the coins. The coins are nothing special. My brother could strike far finer coins. My brother would not allow me to decorate the house with wages. It is best that I work as his striker for no wages. The wages will be reinvested in the forge.

Finally my brother agrees that it is best. He calls me to the anvil. He hangs a leather apron from my neck. He folds my fingers around the handle of the sledge. I lift the sledge. It wobbles. The sledge wobbles but I hold it upright. I am officially my brother's striker. My brother takes the sledge from my hand. He says we should smoke the doctor's cigar in celebration. My brother had set the cigar to dry in the pritchel hole of the anvil. Now it is dry. You would never know the cigar had lain in the water on the floor of the forge. It catches fire just like a cigar. The doctor smoked his first cigar with our father. I am smoking my first cigar with my brother. The end of the cigar crumbles slightly on my lips and I lick my lips and spit like my brother. We go to the double doors of the forge and stand together looking down at the town. I cannot see the doctor's office, but I remember that the doctor's office is on a dead end street. His office is the same faded color as the other offices in town. It is hard to imagine that inside the doctor's office there is new equipment capable of reconstructing the last moments of a person's life.

Ships are moored in the bay. My brother points to the flags that fly from the gaffs. He tells me the flags are called "civil ensigns." The ships are merchant ships from foreign countries. Foreigners are taking an interest in the town. More businesses in the town are thriving and my brother tells me that when a certain number of businesses thrive in a town, opinions of the town are revised. The town is considered a good risk for investors. Each townsperson benefits from investment in his town. My brother says that people in a prosperous town take pride in their work and that their work is held to a higher standard. My brother has not been blacksmith for very long, but his work can be held to the highest standard. He finished our father's final job alone. He has surpassed our father. My brother will not disappoint the foreigners. He deserves to be blacksmith in a prosperous town.

3

In the morning my brother wakes me. I follow him from the house to the forge. I face my brother across the anvil. I did not expect to be my brother's striker. When my brother taps with his hammer, I have to remind myself that I am his striker before I strike with the sledge. My brother is unhappy. I am too slow. I do not always strike where he has indicated. I am grateful that my brother does not have a new job to finish. My slowness would be much worse for my brother if a customer were waiting on my brother's work. My brother wants me to practice with the nail rods. My arms are tired. It takes me five strikes to head each nail. Time after time my brother throws my nails in the scrap pile. My brother calls me to the anvil. He holds the iron on the anvil. He taps. I look at the iron. The anvil is mounted too high. The grips on the tools are too wide. I strike blows where my brother taps. My brother says I can stop. A man has appeared at the double doors. It is the doctor. He carries a packet of papers. They must contain the findings from his new equipment. Our father has yielded such a thick packet of papers. I should not have expected anything less from our father. I try to see if my brother is proud of the papers our father yielded. My brother does not look at me. He is approaching the doctor at the double doors. The doctor gives the packet to my brother. My brother's fingers mark the white pages. He looks at the doctor. The doctor explains that our father had been suffering from a long illness. It is a blessing that our father's suffering is over. A sudden death is a wonderful thing when a man is suffering from a long illness. It is more tragic when a sick man dies slowly from a long illness, or when a healthy man dies suddenly. The doctor wants us to know this was not the case with our father. The doctor thinks my brother does not look well. He offers to run tests on my brother at his office. My brother does not like to leave the forge. He says no to the doctor. I would not have said no to the doctor. The doctor has taken an interest in my brother. My brother is big and strong but unwell. He is exactly what the doctor wants in a patient. My brother does not have time to be a patient. He is rude to the doctor. He throws the packet of papers on the hearth. The doctor's eyes shine as he watches the papers burn on the hearth. His mouth trembles. I am surprised that my brother is so rude. He has assumed responsibility for the forge too young. The responsibility is changing him. My brother turns his back on the doctor. I do not want to defy my brother. I turn my back on the doctor. When I look again the doctor is gone.

I wish I could have interested the doctor. I know that I would be a good patient. The doctor does not think I have what it takes. After my brother's rejection, the doctor will not come to the forge again. I will not have another opportunity to interest the doctor. My brother has spoiled the doctor's visit. The doctor's previous visit was much better. The doctor spoke movingly and my brother behaved appropriately, in a way that the doctor said would make our father proud.

Our father must not have known he was suffering from a long illness. Every day he worked in the forge. He turned the iron and my brother struck the iron with the sledge. My brother lifted the sledge high. He struck the iron in just the right place. Our father's leather apron fit my brother perfectly. Our father turned the iron. He hammered. He plunged the iron in the tub. He never tired. Until my brother, no blacksmith had ever surpassed our father. I pumped the bellows. I swept the floor. I went into town for the meat and the bread. Our father had a huge appetite. Only my brother can eat as much as my father. I always put the meat on the dishes for our father and my brother. Now that I am my brother's striker my brother says I need to eat meat. I need to fill my dish with meat. Otherwise I will not grow. I will not improve as a striker and my brother's work will suffer.

For dinner I fill my dish with meat. I eat the dish of meat. My brother refills his dish. He refills my dish. My brother thinks I have what it takes to be his striker. I am eating meat and soon I will be able to lift the sledge easily. I will lift the sledge high. My brother and I eat the meat without speaking. I cannot speak. The meat is piling up in my throat. The cavity inside my body is filled with meat, but there is more meat on my dish. There is no room in my cavity, but I cannot leave meat on my dish. I take all of the meat from my dish and put it in my mouth. I swallow. Some of the meat remains in my mouth.

My brother sleeps in the bed where our father slept. I sleep in the bed where my brother slept. I store the pallet where I used to sleep beneath my brother's bed, which is now the bed where I sleep. As soon as I lie down the meat begins to push out of my cavity. More and more of the meat comes up from my throat to fill my mouth. Luckily I vomit without noise. I vomit on the floor beside the bed. I reach beneath the bed and grab a corner of the pallet. I pull the pallet over the vomit and slide the pallet back beneath the bed. The vomit slides beneath the bed with the pallet. The pallet is on top of the vomit and the vomit cannot be seen. I am good at hiding the vomit. Not a trace remains on the floor. It is a job well done. I hope I am still holding some of the meat inside. I did my best to finish the meat. I finished the meat. I hope I did not waste all of the meat that I worked so hard to finish. It was a mistake to lie down. If I had remained standing up the meat piled in my throat would have weighed on the meat lower down in my cavity. I should have used the weight of the meat, like my brother says I need to use the weight of the sledge. I am too tired not to lie down after dinner. Maybe I can sleep sitting on the floor with my back against the wall. When I am bigger I will be able to hold more meat. I need to hold the meat inside in order to grow. Next time I will use the weight of the meat to my advantage.

4

Now that I am my brother's striker, there is no helper to pump the bellows and sweep the floors. There is no helper to go into town for the meat and the bread. My brother says he will hire a helper. Until my brother hires a helper, I must perform the old tasks. I am glad I must perform the old tasks. It is too tiring to face my brother across the anvil with the sledge for hours and hours. The pains in my elbows make the tears come to my eyes. Sometimes the tears go down my face. My brother does not say anything. He taps with the hammer and I strike with the sledge. I am grateful he does not comment on the tears on my face. I doubt my brother ever struck the iron with tears on his face. If a customer appeared at the double doors I would be ashamed. The customer might mistake me for my brother's son and I know this mistake would not make my brother proud. No customer appears.

While my brother forges hoes, I go into town for the meat and the bread. I walk along the wharves. I admire the civil ensigns flying from the ships. Two small children are playing mumblety-peg on a stretch of mud. Once I would have wanted to join them but now I am my brother's striker. Our father is dead and I have smoked a cigar. I do not want to join the children. The children beckon for me to play. The blade of their knife is broken. It does not stick in the mud no matter how skillfully they make their throws. I tell the children I have no time for games. I will repair their knife if they bring it to the forge. The children do not believe me. They say I have forfeited the game. They are still the champions of the wharves. They mock me as I walk away. I am looking for the doctor's office. I cannot remember which office is the doctor's office. I remember it is not far from the wharves. Every office in the town looks alike. The façades are identical. North of the wharves is the industrial section of the town. The biggest building is the drapery. The drapery is thriving. In the lot behind the drapery, men load crates onto lorries to take to the wharves. I watch the men load the crates. All of the men are smoking cigars as they work. The men see me watching and shout to me. They offer me a job loading crates. The drapery is thriving. There are too many crates for the men to load onto the lorries. They are behind schedule. I tell the men that I already have a job. I am the striker from the forge on the hill. The men seem impressed. The biggest man offers me a cigar. I am thankful that I already know how to smoke cigars. I smoke the cigar easily. The men drop a crate and it breaks open. Uniforms spill from the crate. The drapery produces uniforms for the soldiers. There are many soldiers stationed along the coast and the draper is a rich man. He pays his manager the highest salary of all the managers in the town. The manager makes sure that the uniforms do not vary from one another in any way except for the sizes. The

drapery produces excellent uniforms between which no varia-
tions can be detected. When the men drop the crates and the
uniforms spill onto the dirty lot, the manager's work is ruined.
The fouled uniforms are unfit for the soldiers. The men get
down on their knees to pick up the uniforms. The manager
appears and begins to abuse the men for their stupidity. I walk
away out of consideration for the men. I finish my cigar in
front of the drapery.

Even though the drapery is thriving, the paint has peeled from
the façade of the drapery. The sign is illegible. The manager
cannot be blamed for the outside condition of the drapery. In
the town, paint peels immediately. Salts draw moisture from
the wood and the moisture pushes the paint off the boards.
The manager will have the drapery repainted soon. My brother
told me that our mother painted the boards alongside the windows of our house. He can remember that the boards looked
bright, although he cannot remember what kind of bright. He
remembers bright like a summer sky, which means they might
have been yellow or blue. I cannot remember the bright boards.
The paint peeled. There are no traces of paint on the boards.
The forge is on the hill above the bay, but the salts travel in the
air. The salts pushed the paint off the boards.

When the blacksmith and his striker are working hard in the
forge on the hill, the ground vibrates. The air vibrates. The salt
shakes out of the air. Unless you see the crystals on the ground
at the end of the day, you know you could have worked harder. The day our father showed my brother the crystals on the
ground was the proudest day of my brother's life. My brother
showed me where the crystals covered the ground. The crystals were deep enough for my brother to leave his tracks. I told
my brother that our father must have poured the salt on the
ground. Our father poured the salt when my brother was not

looking. My brother struck my face. I woke up on the ground. My mouth tasted like iron. The ground was vibrating. The air was vibrating. I lay looking up at the summer sky. The brightness was made of tiny points like crystals. I did not mean to hurt my brother by telling him our father poured the salt on the ground. I do not know why my brother was hurt. I never heard our father tell stories about salt. I would have been happy if our father showed me the salt he poured on the ground. I would not have cared that it did not shake from the air, not if our father had put it on the ground for me to see.

5

After I buy the meat and the bread I think about where to go. I have been gone from the forge for much of the day. It should not have taken so long to buy the meat and the bread. I am very slow. I am developing too slowly. Our father did not take an interest in me. He could tell that I would be slow. I should not be my brother's striker. The striker must surpass the blacksmith. I will never surpass my brother. It is too bad I am his only relative. My brother should have a son. How will my brother have a son? He has taken responsibility for the forge. The forge requires all of his attention. Once my brother has expanded the forge, the forge will require even more attention. If the improvements my brother makes are labor-saving improvements, perhaps the improvements will free up time for my brother. But my brother will have to take responsibility for the labor-saving improvements. This new responsibility will occupy the time freed up by the improvements. My brother will be angry I wasted time looking for the doctor's office. I will tell my brother that there was a long line at the bakery. Foreigners enjoy the pastries typical to our region. The bakery is thriving. The baker has raised the prices. Only the foreigners buy the pastries. Before foreigners began visiting our town, the bakery did not need to bake any pastries. Now the baker bakes more pastries than loaves of bread. The baker raised the price of the loaves of bread so that the loaves of bread cost nearly as much as the pastries. The pastries do not seem expensive when you consider the price of bread.

I return to the wharves. Maybe I will recognize the doctor's dead end street. It is pleasant to walk around by the wharves. Foreigners are eating pastries in the sunshine. Seagulls circle the foreigners. The older foreigners have ivory-topped canes. They threaten the seagulls with their canes. They gesture feebly with their canes. The older foreigners are not so old that they need to gesture so feebly. It is obvious that the older foreigners do not mind the seagulls. The younger foreigners carry notebooks. They take notes in their notebooks. From the expressions on their faces, they consider the town a good risk for investment. They shake pastry crumbs for the seagulls. The fish sellers do not like that the foreigners shake crumbs for the seagulls. Seagulls are a nuisance. The town has an ordinance against feeding the seagulls. The fish sellers will not report the foreigners. The foreigners create small nuisances but they have made the town prosperous. The fish sellers are selling cases of fish to the foreigners. The fish lie in rows on the ice. Their mouths are open. Their eyes and their scales are bright. The fish sellers get a good price for the fish. I had never thought that the town could become prosperous. The faded buildings give the town a dilapidated look. The town is not dilapidated. Paint peels immediately because of the salts. The faded buildings are not neglected. Some of the buildings are new. I do not remember all of these buildings from my previous walks by the wharves. They must be new. The new buildings make it hard for me to find the doctor's street. The foreigners like the dilapidated look of the town. The town is actually quite safe. The dilapidation is typical of the region. It is picturesque and not an impediment to growth.

I wander away from the wharves to the center of the town. The streets are wider in the center of the town. I stand in the middle of the street. I have my back to the bay. Nothing blocks the view of the forge. The crest of the hill is bare. Our father cut the trees for charcoal. There is smoke in the blue sky above the forge. I can hear my brother working high above the town. The sounds travel on the air. I am hungry from my walk. I eat all of the loaf of bread I bought from the baker. I eat standing in the middle of the street. I am very hungry. I look through the display windows of the buildings. One of the buildings displays hammers in the window. The display is of a high quality. Hammers are mounted on hooks that fit through holes in a board. The hammers have different colored handles. Other than the colors of the handles the hammers are the same. The difference between the hammers is purely decorative. I enter the building. It is a hardware store. There are bins of machined nails and bolts. The clerk tries to speak with me. I will not speak to the clerk. I leave the store immediately. It is urgent that I return to the forge, but I have no bread. I go again to the bakery. The doctor enters the bakery as the baker hands me the loaf of bread in a paper bag. I wait for the doctor to make his purchase. The doctor does not look at me. He buys seeded rolls. I am too embarrassed to speak to the doctor, but I follow him back to his office. I pay attention to the turns the doctor makes. The doctor's office is at the end of a dead end street. There are bundles of newspapers outside of the office next door to the doctor's. I do not know how I would have forgotten that the doctor's office is next door to the newspaper office. The newspaper office must have moved. I do not think the newspaper office was located on a dead end street. Now that the doctor has gone into his office the street is empty. I pull a newspaper from a bundle and slide it into the bag with the bread.

6

I retrace my steps to the bakery but I make a mistake. I do not remember this intersection. I choose a street. The streets by the wharves are narrow and winding. I end up back by the bay. Now I am farther from the forge than I was when I followed the doctor to his office. I pass the muddy stretch on the edge of the bay. The knife with the broken blade is lying on the mud. All around the knife the mud is deeply gouged. There must have been a great struggle on the mud, a struggle for the knife. I slide the knife into the bag with the bread. I examine a dead fish on the mud. If its scales were bright I would pry off the scales with the broken blade of the knife, but the scales are dull. I leave the knife in the bag. Something moves by the hull of an overturned boat. A soldier is crouching by the overturned boat. He gestures. I cannot interpret the gesture of the soldier. The gesture must be a command. I hurry to the soldier. I have never seen a soldier crouched by a boat in the mud. The soldier stands as I approach. His hair and beard are very long, and his uniform is all one piece. I realize the soldier is a monk from the peninsula.

The monks from the peninsula make their uniforms out of cloth from the drapery, the same cloth that is cut into the uniforms for the soldiers. Unlike the uniforms of the soldiers, the uniforms of the monks are not cut into shirts and trousers. Their uniforms are all one piece. A soldier would never wear a uniform that was all one piece. Soldiers need uniforms that are two pieces, shirts and trousers. Now that I know that the soldier is a monk, I do not have to obey his gesture. I can walk away. I hope that I was not seen obeying the monk's gesture. The wharves have emptied, but someone could be watching from an office window or from the high deck of a ship. As I turn to walk away from the monk, I notice he is wearing an iron talisman. The talisman looks familiar. I ask the monk about the talisman, but he shakes his head. He is a monk who does not speak. The monk rummages in his sack. He puts a jar of gooseberry jam in my hand. He holds out his hand. I put the jar back in his hand. The monk continues to hold out his hand with the jar balanced on his palm. Even though I look down at the mud, I can tell that the monk is looking at me.

I begin to walk away from the monk. From behind, I hear a high, thin sound. The sound is high enough to make a pain in my ear. I turn. The monk's arm is straight out, the jar balanced on his hand. The monk is screaming. He has not opened his mouth to scream, or he is screaming with his mouth open to a slit that is hidden by his beard. I go and take the jar from the monk. The monk screams louder. He lifts the empty hand to my face. His fingers are curled. I see the long cracked nails with dirt in the cracks. The nails come close to my mouth. The monk screams louder and louder. Someone will think I am abusing the monk. I put the last of my brother's money in the monk's hand. The monk closes his hand around the money. The scream stops. I can still feel air coming out of the monk. The monk is forcing air from his lungs with no sound. I back away. The monk does not move. He looks at me, with his eyes stretched open wide and his mouth hidden by his beard. He lowers his closed hand to his side.

I am so late that I run up the hill. The clanging from the forge is very loud. My brother is working hard. I go into our house. Nothing has moved. My brother did not break for lunch. Two chairs are pushed out from the table. Our father's ledgers are piled at one end of the table. There are two dishes on the table. There is a fork on each dish. I swat the flies from the dishes. I unwrap the meat. I fry strips of meat. I slide the bread from its paper bag. The crust of the bread has grayed with ink from the newspaper. I fry the bread in the grease from the meat. I put the meat and the bread on the dishes. I put most of the meat and bread on my brother's dish. Before I take the dishes to the forge, I remember to take the knife with the broken blade from the bag. I do not want my brother's help repairing the knife. I should be able to repair the knife easily. I hide the knife in my bed between the bed mat and the frame. I realize I have already begun to refer to the knife as the "champion's knife." When I repair the knife I will be the champion of the wharves.

7

My brother is too hungry to ask questions about what I did all day in town. He eats standing up at the anvil. I eat standing at the double doors. I have no difficulty emptying my dish, even though I ate the loaf of bread earlier in the afternoon. I must be growing. I look out at the bay. The sun is low over the bay. The air over the bay contains the highest quantity of salts. My brother told me the air over the bay is so thick with salts the salts cause optical illusions. This is why the sun appears so large over the bay. It is magnified by the prisms of the salts. My brother is wrong. The sun is very large, far larger than it appears over the bay. The sun is larger than the world. Salts in the air must shrink the image of the sun. This is why we see the sun as a disc instead of a burning plane that fills the sky. My brother tries to repeat what our father told him. For the first time I am hearing our father's stories. It must have been different to hear the stories from our father. Our father was never wrong. Something happens to our father's stories when my brother repeats them. They are changed. My brother believes what he repeats. He does not realize there is a difference between the stories he repeats and our father's stories. There must be a difference.

I look out at the bay. The whole sky is bright. The sun is a disc, low and dull in the sky. The brightness of the sky does not come from the disc. The sky and the disc are illusions caused by the salts in the air. Behind them is the burning plane. I can almost see it. I have to open my eyes wide and look toward the outside corner of each eye. Then I can almost see it. No one taught me this skill. I taught myself. I am the only person in the town who can see through the sky. If the doctor ran tests on me in his office, he might discover the physiological basis of this skill. His machines might express the physiological basis of this skill graphically, making finely inked lines. Instead of describing my skill, I could show people a printout from the doctor. Everyone would admire the beautiful waveforms on the printout, waveforms emitted by my brain and inked by the doctor's machines.

My brother comes to make sure I have emptied my dish. I have emptied my dish. It is time to work. My brother takes a leather apron from the nail. He hangs the leather apron from my neck. He has not cut the leather apron to my size like he promised. The skirt of the apron touches the ground. I have to be careful or I will trip. A striker should not trip. It is only excusable to lie on the floor of the forge one time. Our father lay on the floor of the forge one time. He lay on his back and his hair was on fire. His eyelids swelled. His cheeks swelled. The skin on his cheeks split. Fluids ran down the slopes of his cheeks, toward the ears and the chin. My brother doused our father with the water from the tub. Thin black smoke rose from our father's face. My brother sent me to town so I did not have to breathe our father's smoke.

It is difficult to remember faces. To picture our father I look at my brother. When my brother turns his back, I forget how our father looked. I remember our father on his back on the floor. The tip of his nose had been burned away on the coals. There was a hole in our father's nose. It was big enough to hold a cigar. That was not how our father's face looked. Our father's face was changed by the hearth. Only his hands were unchanged. They were big, with dirty grains in the skin. The doctor put our father's hand on his chest. He put the cigar in our father's hand. According to the doctor, this was a natural pose for our father, the pose of our father as a small boy on the wharves. Our father always held a cigar or a knife on the wharves with the doctor. The doctor remembered our father best in this pose.

8

A storm must have blown in from the ocean after dark. The sky is dense and black. In the flashes of lightning, the dark skin beneath my brother's eyes looks burned. His lips look burned. He banks the fire for the night. In the house, he eats cold meat from the pan. I open the newspaper. I find the obituary for our father. I had not known the date our father was born. I say the date to my brother. My brother already knew the date. He says he has the same birthday as our father. My brother tells me the year he was born. I do the figures in my head. Our father was exactly the age my brother is now when my brother was born. I did not realize our father had my brother so young. My brother does not say anything more. I wonder if he is doing the figures in his head.

I read our father's obituary to my brother. I am not mentioned in our father's obituary as a survivor of our father. My brother says newspapers have limited space for obituaries. It is not practical to list every survivor. My brother is our father's survivor. My brother says he is glad he is listed. The only difference between our father and my brother is the year they were born. The year my brother was born is not mentioned in the obituary. Only my brother's name is mentioned. When they read my brother's name in our father's obituary, people will see that there is no difference between the deceased and the survivor. There has been no interruption in service at the forge. My brother does not recognize the address for the memorial service. I tell him it is the address of the doctor's office. My brother has no interest in going to the doctor's office for the memorial service. He says it is not appropriate for the survivor to be in the same place as the deceased.

Before I go to bed my brother wants me to put him in my mouth. He opens his pants and turns his chair to the side. If he did not turn his chair to the side I would have had to crawl under the table to reach my brother. I rest one hand on the edge of my brother's chair and one hand on the table. I wish my mouth were not so small and dry. My brother is patient with me, but he is disappointed. He has to use his hand while I crouch by the chair.

Lying in bed, I cannot fall asleep. I took longer than I should have near the wharves and my brother had to use his hand. I do not know how to improve myself. If I had followed the doctor into his office perhaps he would have given me one of his capsules. The doctor would not have given me a capsule. Doctors only offer capsules to their patients. He might have given me a capsule for my brother. I decide to stay up all night so I will be awake before my brother in the morning. I will be ready to go to work in the forge. I wake up with a start when my brother shakes my shoulder. He has already fried the meat for breakfast. The air through the windows is salty and fresh with last night's storm.

9

My brother does not know why there are no customers. He dresses three axes. He forges hoe after hoe. He paces to the double doors of the forge. It is a clear day. On clear days, you can see the peninsula across the bay, the faint gray outline of the mountains. My brother calls to me. He can see the peninsula. I join him at the double doors. The day is exceptionally clear. I can see the stone monasteries set high on the mountains. The peninsula is long and thin. It stretches across the horizon. I do not know where the peninsula attaches to the coast. It must attach some place far away, in the wilderness to the south. The peninsula is not continuous. There are breaks in the peninsula through which ships enter the bay. The ships in the bay fly bright civil ensigns. They have come from far away, across the ocean. They move very quickly through the waters of the bay. The foreigners like to cross the bay at alarming speeds. The speeding ships make crossing from the peninsula to the town dangerous for the monks. The boats of the monks are crudely built, with low sides, and they take on water when they cross the rough waves of the bay. The monks build laughable boats. It is a miracle that their boats stay afloat on the bay.

The foreigners play a game with the monks. The captains of the ships try to drive their ships over the boats of the monks. The foreigners gather on the decks of the ships. They laugh. They look down to the water to see if there are small boats tossing in the wakes of the ships. Monks wash up by the wharves of the town. The doctor's practice is thriving. He has more and more opportunities to use his medical equipment. It is too bad all of the monks died in the same way. It must not be challenging for the doctor. I am sure that the monks do not produce big packets of paper like our father. The monks do not even receive obituaries in the newspaper. Instead there is a tally, a tally of the monks who have washed up by the wharves. This is how the foreigners keep score. Games with the monks keep the captains of the ships from becoming bored in a town as small as ours.

I tell my brother about the monk I saw by the wharves. The monk had not washed up by the wharves. He was lucky and had not lost the game to a captain. He had arrived alive by the wharves of the town. He did not lie face down. He crouched by his boat on the mud. I describe the iron talisman. My brother is not surprised by my description. He says the monks make their own talismans. There is a forge on the peninsula. A long time ago, the man who sold our father's father the forge left the town for the peninsula. He became a monk. He built a new forge on the peninsula. He taught the monks to forge talismans. The monks know how to work iron thanks to the man who sold our father's father the forge.

10

My brother closes the double doors of the forge. I look at the iron door pulls. They are the same as the monk's talisman. That is why the monk's talisman looked familiar. I feel close to the monks now that I know their talismans are modeled on the pulls of the double doors.

The man who sold our father's father the forge had lost his family to a disease. They could not keep any fluids inside their bodies and even their skin lost its moisture and shrank. It was a common disease. The man buried his family behind the forge. He had no living relatives and so he no longer had any hope for the future of the forge. My brother says that is why the man sold our father's father the forge. He did not care that our father's father changed the name of the forge. The man's name was no longer important. He decided to become a monk on the peninsula. Monks do not have names. They are called brothers. Brother is how they greet each other unless they have taken a special vow. In that case, they exchange only gestures when they meet.

Before the town became prosperous, it was common for men to lose hope. It was good that the peninsula was so close to the town, right across the waters of the bay. Men could leave the town for the peninsula. All they needed was to build a small boat. Speeding ships did not drive over small boats in the bay. The men arrived safely on the peninsula. The monks would welcome the newcomers, even though the newcomers had no hope for the future. Monks do not have sons. If the monks did not welcome newcomers, they would not be able to replace the monks who have died. The order of monks would dwindle. Nobody would inhabit the monasteries on the mountains. The monasteries would become dens for animals, the wild boars that live on the peninsula. Rose bushes would fill the lower stories, the branches would crack the panes of glass in the windows, they would grow through the windows. The windows would become bright with the hips and flowers of roses and the jagged pieces of broken glass. The monasteries are definitely inhabited. The windows are dark.

Now that the foreigners have come, every townsperson benefits from investments in his town. Men no longer lose hope. They do not build small boats to cross the bay. Only the monks cross the bay in small boats. Sometimes the monks take young boys from town back to the peninsula in their boats. By welcoming newcomers and taking young boys, the order of monks has prevented itself from dwindling. Now that there are no newcomers arriving on the peninsula, the monks must take as many young boys as they can. Luckily, the captains play games with the monks and most of the monks arrive face down by the wharves. Those monks cannot take young boys. Instead, they are taken by the doctor, taken to his office at the end of the dead end street.

I wonder if the monks can see our forge from their monasteries on the peninsula. Nothing blocks the view of the forge. The monks must be able to see the red light across the bay. We cannot see the red light of the monks' forge, but the monks' forge might be located on the other side of the monasteries, facing the ocean, or it might be located near the bottom of a ravine.

There are stories of monks taking the young boys from the town in their boats and devouring them down in the ravines of the peninsula. I do not believe these stories. The boys who are taken by the monks must be kept alive so that they can receive instruction. It is important that the next generation of monks learns how to make the jams and the talismans and the boats. If the monks devoured the boys, there would be no young monks to carry on the practices and beliefs of the order. The practices and beliefs of the monks might involve devouring boys, but I do not think the order could have lasted so long if that were the case. Beneath his hair and beard, the monk I saw by the overturned boat did not seem old. Not too long ago he may have been a boy in the town.

11

Today is the first of the month. If our father were alive he would go to deposit the heavy bag of money in the bank. My brother gave the heavy bag of money to the doctor. My brother has nothing to deposit in the bank. For as long as my brother can remember our father deposited money in the bank on the first of the month. This month my brother will have to take money out of the bank to buy the iron for the forge. As I work with my brother, I think about the hardware store. If my brother took just a little extra money from the bank to buy paint, I could carve handles for his axes and paint the handles. Our axes could compete with any axes sold in the hardware store.

I make more mistakes at the anvil than ever before. My brother throws down his hammer. He asks if I am thinking about a girl I saw in town. I am surprised. My brother does not throw his tools or speak about girls in town. He is in a peculiar mood. His face is pale despite the heat of the forge. His lips are dark. I tell my brother that I am thinking about the hardware store. My brother has not heard about the hardware store. He grabs my arms and shakes me while I tell him everything I remember. I do not remember the hours or the prices. I tell him about the different colored handles on the hammers. I tell him about my plan to paint different colored ax handles, bright ax handles in as many colors as the handles of the hammers. My brother shakes me hard so my teeth close on my tongue. Blood comes from between my lips. My brother rubs his shirtsleeve against my mouth. He brushes my hair from my forehead. He says it is not my fault. It is not my fault that no customers come to the forge.

The forge is not in a good location. It is strenuous to travel up the hill to the forge. The path is steep. There is no shade on the hill. Customers never minded traveling up the hill to the forge but now the town is prosperous. In a prosperous town, customers do not want to travel up the hill. By the wharves, the foreigners are building new storefronts. They have built a new district by the wharves, with stores and hotels. The foreigners stay in their district. They stay close to their ships. They do not like to walk through the town even as far as the bakery. Foreigners have been attacked on their walks to the bakery. Now the foreigners have their own bakeries in the district by the wharves. The town is not as safe as it once was. There is more theft in a prosperous town. There are more things to be thieved. The townspeople have begun to shop in the foreigner's district. The foreigners have hired soldiers to patrol their district. It is pleasant to shop without fearing the thieves.

My brother is certain that some of the new storefronts in the foreign district are still unoccupied. My brother could rent a storefront in the foreign district. If my brother could rent a storefront he could display his metalwork in a good location. Customers could purchase andirons at the storefront. They could drop off their tools for repair. I could pick up the tools each week and my brother could repair them at the forge. I could bring the repaired tools back to the storefront and collect the money from the locked box my brother would mount on a heavy piling by the storefront. The locked box and the heavy piling would be unnecessary precautions. Soldiers would protect the money we made at the storefront. Foreigners would pay the soldiers to protect my brother's investment.

My brother becomes excited by this idea. This is one way to expand, opening a storefront in the foreign district in the town. The location of the forge would no longer hinder my brother's success. My brother smiles at me and I smile at my brother. I smile with my lips closed to hide the blood on my teeth. My brother picks up his hammer. He says we can put my ax handles in the display window of the storefront. Maybe I will be good at painting handles. My brother looks thoughtful as he says this. He is wondering what I am good at. I am not a good striker. My brother does not say I am not a good striker. He spoke in a great rush uncommon for him and now he is done with speaking. He does not say anything more. Soon the sounds of hammer and sledge make conversation impossible. I know my brother is thinking I am not a good striker. My sledge hits off-center on the iron. I strike with the sledge again and again. My arms hurt. My back hurts. I cannot hit the right place. I have not grown. My improvement is too slow. I cannot strike the iron where my brother indicates. Now that business is slow my brother can fix my mistakes but when he expands the forge he will not have time to fix my mistakes. I need to improve more quickly. I am good at some things surely, but

what does it matter if I am not a good striker, if I cannot do
the thing my brother needs.

12

My brother has used up our father's bar iron and rods. My brother's metalwork is stacked against the inside walls of the forge. It is very impressive. I wish customers would come to the forge to praise my brother and buy high-quality tools for their homes and businesses. Now my brother has only scrap metal to work with. He cannot make high-quality tools from scrap iron. He must go to town to take out money from the bank. That way he will be able to purchase fresh bar iron for his high-quality products.

Without iron to work, we have nothing to do in the forge. My brother and I sit on the hill watching the ships. My brother says the ships come from the ports of distant cities. He says I cannot possibly imagine the foreigners' cities. There are many more girls in these cities and they are nothing like the girls in town. My brother asks me to describe the girls in town. When I was our father's helper, I went into town more often for the meat and the bread. I must have passed many girls. Girls must walk on the streets in town. They wear uniforms that are all one piece, like the monks. I do not remember if I saw girls or monks on my trips into town. Girls and monks wear their hair very long, but the monks have long beards. The uniforms of the girls are shorter than the uniforms of the monks. This is not the description that my brother wants to hear. I pluck at the grass with my fingers. The sun is hot and the ground buzzes with insects. The buzzing is almost like the vibrations that pass through the ground from the forge when my brother or our father is hard at work.

I tell my brother that I talked to girls in town. We talked many times. The girls were impressed to hear that I worked in the forge. They have great admiration for the blacksmith. The girls asked me to describe the blacksmith using physical detail. I told the girls every physical detail I could remember but the girls were not satisfied. They kept asking for more. My brother does not believe me. He knows I did not talk to any girls in town. He asks me to describe the girls using physical details. I try to think of physical details. My brother leans back on the hill with his hands folded behind his head. I could say that the girls have long hair like the monks. Their uniforms are too short. Girls must grow quickly. My brother has shut his eyes, waiting. I do not know what to say. I touch my brother through his pants but he rolls over. He tightens his buttocks and rubs himself on the earth. He gets on his knees and opens his pants. He opens his eyes and looks at me. He is angry that I am still there. I go into the house and sit on my bed but there is a bad smell so I sit in the doorway. I cannot see my brother or the bay. I look at the back of the forge. Mice live in the scrap metal piled behind the forge. They must be mice, gray flickers in the curving darkness between the prongs.

I do not know the physical details of the girls in town but I know the physical details of my brother. He is the same size as our father. Our father was shorter than my brother but our father had a great chest like a barrel. My brother is taller than our father but his chest is like a slab, flatter and not as big around as our father's. I think their slightly different shapes make them just the same size. My brother has the same swing as our father. The anvil is mounted at the perfect height for both our father and my brother. My brother has dark hair on his backside. His toenails grow in mounds. Everywhere on my brother's body there are red marks where the skin stretched because my brother grew so quickly. His big muscles made marks on his skin as they grew. My brother grew more quickly than the girls in town. Not one of them is big enough to bear his son. If my brother had had a son when my father died, that son would already be big enough to work as my brother's striker. My brother's son could replace me at the anvil. It would not take my brother's son years to grow. He would grow even more quickly than my brother. It would take no time at all for my brother's son to stand at the anvil. He would crawl from his mother's legs to the anvil and rise, holding the sledge in his hand.

13

My brother eats looking over our father's ledgers. He does not notice that I have not emptied my dish. I try to empty my dish but my throat has narrowed. Even the smallest bites of meat lodge in my throat. I leave the table and sit on my bed with my dish. I push the meat off my dish onto the floor. I pull the pallet over the meat. I slide the pallet beneath the bed. Now my dish is empty. I put the empty dish on the floor. I lie down on the bed. I am tired but I cannot fall asleep. I will go outside. I take the saltcellar from the table. My brother does not look up from the ledgers. I leave the house and walk around the hill in the moonlight. I sit down on the hill. The moon illuminates the ships in the bay. Dark figures are moving on the decks of the ships. The foreigners like to dance on the decks of their ships. Their ships are taller than any of the buildings in town. The foreigners are building hotels in their district that will be as tall as the ships. Soon the view of the bay will be blocked by hotels.

Only the foreigners who stay at hotels will see the foreigners who dance on the ships.

I lie back. I balance the saltcellar on my stomach so it points up from my stomach at the moon. I rock from side to side by flexing each buttock. I want to see how far I can rock before the saltcellar topples. The saltcellar topples. Now I can flex each buttock with all of my strength. The burning I feel in my buttocks makes my legs tighten, my stomach tighten. I curl my fingers and toes. I relax my buttocks. I pick up the saltcellar and pour salt on the earth where my brother rubbed. I do not turn over like my brother. I stay on my back. I move my eyes toward the outside corners and look through the disc of the moon to see the bigger, brighter light it hides from my view.

This is the first time I have slept outside. I wake up when the sun is rising. The grass is wet. My body is wet. I feel cold. The bay is covered with mist. I have grown so much in the night that I cannot fit through the door of the house. I cannot fit through the double doors of the forge. I lift the roof off the forge and look inside. My brother is working in his leather apron. I see the bellows and the hearth and my brother at the anvil and the workbenches and the metalwork stacked against the walls. My brother passes up a sledge. He wants me to work at the anvil, but I am too large. I crush the sledge in my fist. Fragments fall. The head of the sledge cracks the brick of the hearth. I reach my arm into the forge. I take the horn of the anvil between my fingertips. I pluck anvil and post from the floor of the forge. I look at the bay. The mist is burning off and I see that the ships in the bay are anvils, gray anvils mounted on the muddy verge of the bay. Instead of civil ensigns, the anvils fly flags that bear the name of the forge. I shout down to my brother. I describe the anvils on the bay and their different colored flags. Each flag bears the same name. It is the proudest moment of my life. We have expanded the forge.

My buttocks tighten with joy. I rock. My buttocks burn. I feel hard irregularities beneath my buttocks. I am standing up, looking out at the bay, but I am also lying down, feeling hard irregularities with my buttocks. Suddenly I am dizzy, sensing myself upright, then supine, upright then supine. My breathing comes in gasps. I roll over and heave, but only air comes out of my throat. The air is hard as rock and hurts me as it pushes from my cavity. I push the rocks of air from my throat. When I am finished, I stumble to the house. The air is gray and damp. I hesitate at the door of the house because I remember having grown. I fit easily through the door. My brother is sitting at the table. He has been sitting there all through the night. I cannot tell if his eyes are opened or closed. As I climb into bed my heart hammers in threes, three quick hammers, the blacksmith's signal that the striker must stop. I realize I am holding a rock in my hand.

14

In case customers come while my brother is down at the bank, I stay at the forge. I do not mind. It is a good opportunity to repair the champion's knife. Often at night my brother leaves the fire alive in the hearth, banked under ashes. This morning the fire is out. I shovel coal on the old fire, two shovelfuls of the good wet coal my brother uses so sparingly. I mix pine twigs with the coal. I light the fire and pump the bellows. The fire is dark and big. The smell is strong. The fire is unwell. The smell fills the forge. I have forgotten the champion's knife. I run to the house. The door is closed, the windows are closed. The air inside the house smells bad.

The champion's knife is changed when I pull it from between the bed mat and frame. It is not a knife at all. It is a broken file. There is no cutting edge on the file. I am certain the champion's knife was a knife. It has changed. My brother must have taken the champion's knife and replaced it with a broken file. I should be able to make the file into the champion's knife. I have never been in the forge without my brother or our father. I like the way the fire smells, strong and unwell. I grind both sides of the file. I put the file in the fire. When the file is red, I take the file from the fire. I drop it in the tub. Maybe I should have bent the file over the horn of the anvil and hammered the file. The file is not shaped exactly like a knife. It is better than a knife because it does not have a handle. I will carve and paint the handle for the champion's knife. I will paint the handle yellow or blue.

Standing at the double doors of the forge, I see the doctor coming up the hill. The doctor moves quickly as though he is in a great hurry. The doctor is thin but he moves quickly. Doctors must be thin and quick. They are summoned in the early morning or late at night and they always respond quickly to the summons. The doctor is busier and busier in town. The town is prosperous and the doctor's practice is thriving. I remember leading the doctor to the forge. I remember following the doctor through the streets between the bakery and the doctor's office. I had difficulty keeping up. The doctor was almost running, his black doctor's bag in one hand, the white baker's bag of seeded rolls in the other.

The doctor's face is beaded with sweat. There is no shade on the hill and the path is steep. The doctor comes right up to the double doors. He wipes his face with a white cloth from his vest pocket. He is looking for my brother. He peers around me into the forge. The ground does not vibrate, the air does not vibrate, no sounds come from the forge, but the doctor expects to see my brother. He does not know my brother at all. Even using his medical equipment, the doctor will never know anything about my brother if he does not know to listen as he approaches the forge.

When I tell the doctor that my brother has gone to town to buy iron, the doctor shakes his head. My brother should not go to town without making an appointment to see the doctor. If my brother made an appointment, he could buy iron and also stop by the doctor's office for tests. Even though the doctor is thriving and has expanded his practice by opening a new office in the foreign district, he would most like to have my brother for a patient. Only then would he feel challenged, as though he were growing as a doctor. A doctor wants the best possible patients. That is how a doctor grows. The doctor lowers his voice so I step closer to the doctor. I cough. The doctor laughs. He has been cleaning his medical equipment with a powerful solvent. He tells me that the smell of the solvent makes some people cough. He sniffs at his wrists, nodding to indicate that he detects the smell of the solvent. I am happy that I am sensitive to the doctor's solvent and that the doctor has confirmed my sensitivity. He is looking at me with bright eyes. I cough again. My sensitivity is of interest to the doctor.

The doctor sets his black doctor's bag on the ground and opens the golden clasp. He takes a newspaper clipping from his bag. He has clipped our father's obituary for my brother. The doctor waves away my thanks as he hands me the clipping. I want the doctor to know that I will not burn the clipping on the hearth. I blow on the clipping with my lips to remove any powders and I press the clipping flat on my chest and smooth its creases. What else can I do to show the doctor that I cherish his clipping? The doctor does not seem satisfied. He paces just outside the double doors of the forge. He links his hands behind his back. I am impressed by the doctor's pacing. The sun is strong but he paces quickly. Sweat beads on the doctor's face. If the doctor will wait until sundown my brother will return from the town. I am certain he will bring the meat and the bread and we can prepare dinner for the doctor. I will give the doctor my portion. If the doctor takes an interest in me, it will not matter what I eat. I will become the doctor's patient. I will grow more quickly under his care.

The doctor cannot be persuaded to wait until sundown. He is disappointed in my brother. He is disappointed that my brother did not come to his office for the memorial service. It would have been right for my brother to hear the doctor eulogize our father. At the memorial service, the doctor said many kind things about our father. He shared anecdotes about our father that my brother should have heard. He talked about playing mumblety-peg with our father, about how our father always threw the knife skillfully. Every time the blade stuck deep in the mud. Our father was impressive to the woman the doctor loved. Our father took the woman from the doctor because he thought it would be amusing to have the woman. After our father made love to the woman the doctor could not satisfy her. No man could satisfy the woman but our father.

I want to know the physical details about the woman but I do not want to interrupt the doctor. The doctor talks on and on. He never pauses. He already knows everything he wants to say because he said it once before, at the memorial service. Finally I interrupt the doctor. I do not ask about the woman. I ask the doctor if he can help me to grow. I tell the doctor that I eat meat. I work hard in the forge. Nothing has improved me. My hands are still too small to grip the sledge efficiently. The doctor examines my hands. I have never been examined by a doctor. The doctor's hands are very cool and smooth. The doctor says my hands are not getting enough blood. There may be a blockage or there may be too much blood going somewhere else. He asks me if I masturbate. I know what the doctor means. I feel the blood move suddenly in my neck and face.

I shake my head like I do not understand. It is believable that I do not understand. No one has ever said that word to me before, but I understand the word. I see the doctor's thin lips shape the word and I understand. I shake my head. The doctor comes closer. This time I do not cough. I hold my breath. The doctor squeezes me through my pants. He taps me through my pants with the tips of his fingers. He bends so that his ear, cheek, and jaw press against the front of my pants. I rest my weight against the doorframe but the doctor straightens up and takes me by the shoulders. I am almost as tall as the doctor. I must be stronger than the doctor, but I cannot break his grip on my shoulders. The doctor makes me stand up, supporting my own weight. He reaches into his black bag and takes out a jar. He smears the contents on his hands. He tells me to lower my pants. I lower my pants. The doctor tells me to walk into the forge and I turn and walk very slowly so I do not trip in my pants. I hear the doctor's brisk steps behind me then I feel him behind me. He pinches my wrists with his fingers and lifts my arms away from my sides. He puts my hands on the anvil. He moves his arm back and forth between my legs until I set my feet far apart. It is hotter by the anvil. The fire I made in the hearth is too big. Smoke makes my eyes tear. The fire is unwell. The air smells strong. I look at my small hands on the anvil. Sweat rolls down the insides of my arms. It is hard to breathe the smoke. I breathe. The doctor says there is no blockage.

15

When my brother returns from town, he does not have the meat or the bread for dinner. I am lying on the grass outside of the forge. I prop myself up on my elbow when I hear my brother call. He calls to me. I see my brother's empty hands, dirty and big, hanging by his sides. I do not call back to my brother. I do not ask about the meat or the bread. I have never seen my brother look so defeated. His big hands are trembling. It is strange to look at my brother standing up in his clothing without the leather apron. Across the anvil, my brother stands with the leather apron hanging down in one brown piece. It covers his shirt and trousers. As my brother approaches, I look at his shirt and trousers. The two fabrics meet along a line that crosses my brother's abdomen. My brother's abdomen is a slab with light and dark fabrics dividing it in two. He sits down beside me on the grass. He does not want to tell me his news, then he tells me his news.

There will be no delivery of bar iron to the forge. We do not have money in the bank. My brother says that he now understands our father's ledgers. Our father was not depositing money for safekeeping in the bank. He was paying the bank each month so that the bank would allow him to work in the forge. We had always believed that our father owned the forge. Our father did not own the forge. The bank owns the forge.

Tears come to my brother's eyes because he finally understands the ledgers. He had not cried when our father died. Then my brother thought he was our father's survivor. Our father's name survived in the forge. The forge survived because my brother was blacksmith. My brother's good work would carry on the good name of the forge. My brother had no reason to cry. Now he knows that the forge should not be called by our father's name. The name is really the same as the name of the bank.

My brother had seen two soldiers stationed by the outer doors of the bank and two soldiers stationed inside, one on either end of the tellers' long counter. At first my brother felt surprise when he saw the soldiers. Before the town became prosperous there was no need to guard the bank. Now the bank must be guarded. More and more money goes in and out of the bank. When thieves leave their strongholds in the wilderness in the south, they travel north until they reach a prosperous town. Before, the thieves used to pass by our town. The dilapidated buildings of the town could not interest the thieves. Now the thieves note signs of prosperity. The buildings in the town are faded, but civil ensigns fly from the ships in the bay. Tall buildings are being erected in the foreign district. Thieves can see these tall buildings from far away, from far down the coast. The thieves head straight to our town. They target the foreigners' investments. The soldiers have been stationed at the bank to keep the investments safe. They have received orders to shoot any thieves on sight. In a prosperous town, thieves are recognizable. It is easy for the soldiers to shoot the thieves.

My brother stood behind the draper in the line at the bank. The draper was depositing large bags of money. He seemed pleased to see the soldiers stationed at either end of the tellers' counter in their clean, smartly ironed uniforms. The draper is happy that the soldiers take such good care of his uniforms. The draper does not have to worry that the soldiers will be too careful with the uniforms, so careful that he will not need to produce more. Every time a soldier is injured or killed, his uniform is spoiled. No matter how careful a soldier may be, eventually he will either spoil his uniform or he will attain a new rank. When soldiers attain new ranks, they qualify for new uniforms. When soldiers are injured or killed, they are replaced by new soldiers who require uniforms. The draper could not be happier. There is no end to the demand for soldiers' uniforms. If he ever lost his contract with the agency responsible for providing uniforms to soldiers, he would kill himself at once. The life that the draper used to lead before he won his contract is so incomparable to his life today that they cannot be considered the same thing. They cannot both be called life. Killing himself is the closest thing he can imagine to his old life. He said as much to my brother. My brother asked the draper to say the name of the bank. The draper said that foreigners had bought the bank. The name is completely foreign, too foreign to be said aloud. Soon the bank will be moved to the foreign district where a greater number of soldiers will be stationed outside and inside the doors. They will do an even better job protecting the bank.

16

I wonder if my brother has no hope. Sitting beside me on the hill with his hands by his sides, he looks as though he has no hope. The man who sold our father's father the forge had no hope after he lost his family to a common disease. Our father's father bought the forge. Our father's father had hope. He built our house behind the forge, where the man had buried his family. He built our house right on top of the man's deceased family. He had our father. Right away, he knew that our father would surpass him as blacksmith. Our father also had hope. He had my brother. Right away, he knew that my brother would surpass him as blacksmith. Our father had hope until the end, when he lay down on the floor of the forge. He had lost his name but he continued to work in the forge with his son. He knew that his son would work hard until he earned back his name.

My brother tells me he will work even harder so that he can buy the forge from the bank. He will earn back our father's name. The sun is setting. In the house, there is only enough food for my brother. I do not mind. I am not hungry. I do not tell my brother that the doctor came to see him and made me his patient. It is better my brother does not know the doctor came. My brother has no interest in the doctor. The doctor is not a customer. The doctor never brings his tools to the forge for repair. He travels by ship to conferences where he purchases new tools. He brings only paper to the forge. My brother does not have time to think about the doctor. While my brother looks through my father's ledgers I feel between the bed mat and the frame for my clipping of our father's obituary. I crumple it into my pocket. I place the doctor's clipping between the bed mat and the frame, flattening it carefully so it does not tear. I only need one clipping of our father's obituary. I prefer that I have the doctor's clipping. I will put my old clipping on the coals on the hearth.

17

When I go into the forge in the morning, my brother is holding the champion's knife. He is looking at the champion's knife. I make a noise and he notices that I am standing in the double doors. My brother smiles. He asks me if I want to play mumblety-peg. My brother has never asked me to play mumblety-peg. The children play mumblety-peg down by the wharves. Even as a small boy my brother did not throw knives at the mud. He wielded the sledge. He struck the iron wherever our father indicated. My brother's voice is not friendly as he asks me if I want to play mumblety-peg. I do not answer. My brother throws the knife at the anvil. It flips once in the air and breaks apart against the horn of the anvil. I do not move. My brother picks up the largest piece of the champion's knife. The fracturing of the champion's knife has caused my brother pain. He shakes his head. He does not understand how it is possible that I failed to make something as simple as a knife. My brother tosses the piece onto the hearth. The fire on the hearth is already hot. The champion's knife lands in the center of the coals. My brother shovels more coals on top, burying it. That is the end of the champion's knife.

It is difficult to work. I cannot look at the iron on the anvil without seeing my hands on the anvil, my hands where the doctor put them on the anvil. My brother taps. He taps. He turns the iron. I need to concentrate on the iron my brother turns. I need to concentrate on sending blood to my hands as I swing with the sledge. My hands need blood to grow. My muscles need blood. It is difficult to think about the iron and the blood at the same time. They have the same taste, but the iron is hard on the anvil and blood is fluid, like iron that has melted on the hearth, remaining too long beneath the coals. The champion's knife will melt beneath the coals. The champion's knife could run through my veins. If it cooled inside my veins, my veins would harden. My body would be hard and strong. It could be shaped with a few quick blows of the sledge. My body could be sharpened.

I look at my brother's throat above the apron. His throat is big and dark. It shines with my brother's sweat. I could press my sharpened arm against his throat and the skin would part. The darkness inside his throat would spill out. It would run over my arm. My brother's head would fall from his shoulders and land on the floor of the forge. I do not want to see my brother without his head. I am surprised that I can think of such a terrible thing. My brother's head is filled with blood and if his head were not attached to his body, the blood would cool. It would harden. My brother's head would be heavy and would yield too many nails to count. I would make his head into all kinds of nails and sell them for a good price. My brother would be proud. It is easy to think about blood and iron when I remember that there is no difference between them. A person's heart is the hearth that heats the blood. There is no difference between heart and hearth.

At midday my brother lays his hammer on the workbench. He eats a heel of bread on the grass outside the double doors. I want to rest on my stomach so the sun does not shine on my face but my brother does not want me to rest. I sit upright with back against an open door and my legs straight out. My brother wants to share his idea and it is important that I am not resting when I hear it. The idea came to my brother in the night. It was a vision of his walk to the bank along the wharves. Walking to the bank along the wharves, my brother had noticed the chains that moored the ships in the bay. Up close, the chains were big, bigger than he had imagined. They were the biggest chains that existed. My brother had noticed rust on the chains. In the vision, my brother saw the rust growing, moving rapidly over the links of the chain. The iron curded all over with rust. The chains crumbled. The waves in the bay were orange with rust. My brother is thankful for the vision. It means the chains will need to be repaired soon. My brother will get a contract from the foreigners. The contract will ensure that my brother repairs the chains for the ships. It should not be impossible to secure such a contract. The draper is not the only man in the town who has the right to a contract.

Repairing hardware for such large ships will be a bigger job than ever before. Even our father would not have dreamed of such a job. When my brother gets a contract to forge hardware for the foreigners' ships, the forge will thrive. My brother will expand the forge. He will double the forge. My brother cannot be responsible for two forges, not if he is the only blacksmith. It is good to have a brother. Two brothers can be blacksmiths at two forges, two forges that have the same name. The forges are two halves of the same forge. The way my brother is talking, the foreigners' contract will double the forge in a very short period of time. I will be a blacksmith soon. My brother is happy talking about his contract. He looks toward the bay while he talks, toward the ships moored in the bay. The draper is a happy man thanks to his contract with the agency responsible for providing uniforms to soldiers and my brother will be a happy man thanks to his contract with the foreigners.

My brother cannot fulfill the terms of his contract alone. He needs a striker who can soon become a blacksmith in the other half of the doubled forge. Suddenly my brother cries out, a hoarse yell, and he throws his body against me so that I am slammed hard against the open door. The hoarse yell dies quickly into the soundless air on the top of the hill. The door bangs against the forge and the hinges creak. My brother's hands grip my arms. His fingers completely encircle my arms. My arms are the same size around as the grips on the handles of my brother's tools. I could be a tool for my brother but I cannot be his striker. I am too small. I do not fight my brother. I go limp. My brother's body is hot and wet with sweat and it presses against my body. He puts his forehead on my forehead. His breath makes my face drip. My brother releases my arms and pushes my head with his hands. He is smoothing and tugging the hair on my head with his wet forehead hard on the ridges of my brows. My face drips. It is hard to move my mouth and speak into my brother's face, but I speak. I tell my brother that the doctor came to visit. He examined me and made me his patient. Under the doctor's care I will grow quickly. I will soon have what it takes to be a blacksmith. My brother flops to the side and the hot, bright air goes between our bodies. I draw up my knees. My face is dripping with fluids. My brother wipes his nose with the back of his hand. He touches my arm with his knuckles. He wants to believe that I will grow quickly. So far nothing has helped me to grow quickly. Maybe the doctor will help. My brother does not want me to cry. He squeezes my shoulder with his gentlest grip, a grip that is much stronger than the doctor's.

18

In town, there is a lawyer who can draw up contracts. His office is next to the bank. Before my brother leaves to see the lawyer, he eats the last of the onions fried in butter. It is a bad breakfast, onions fried in butter. I use a lot of butter because the onion is small. My brother's lips are covered with grease, and his fingers. He pretends to be angry that his fingers are covered with so much grease. As he goes out the door of the house, he wipes his fingers clean on the front of my pants. He laughs. His touch is rough and I feel it through my pants. The blood goes to where he touches.

Alone in the forge, I stir the cold ashes on the hearth with the tongs. I feel a hard shape. I think it is the live coals beneath the ashes, but the shape is not coal. It is the champion's knife. I take hold of the champion's knife with the tongs. The metal has melted into a twisted lump, like the boll of a tree. I trim two handspans of apron string from the leather apron and make a cord to hang the lump around my neck. No blacksmith has ever forged such a lump. It is an entirely unfamiliar talisman. Even the children on the wharf would not recognize this talisman for what it was.

My brother returns with two other men who beat the ass that walks between them. The ass pulls a lorry of bar iron. My brother and the men are having a fine conversation, laughing and winking. I watch them from the top of the hill. When they arrive at the even ground in front of the forge I run behind to the house. It is cooler in the house and I throw myself on my stomach on the bed. There is a bad smell but I do not mind. I would rather smell the bad smell from beneath the bed than hear the jokes of my brother and the men. My brother does not miss my help unloading the iron. He does not shout for me. I had expected him to shout and so I let the door of the house stand open. I wanted to be sure to hear my brother's shout, to respond slowly to my brother's shout, to make him wait for my help. He does not shout. Finally I go to the forge. I step over the ass dung on the grass. The men are gone. The bar iron is stacked against the walls inside the forge. My brother is arranging tools on the workbench. He gives me a piece of bread from the white bag on the workbench. I will need to be strong for the job, the job on which the future of the forge depends.

In exchange for the help with the contract, the lawyer wants my brother to make bars to protect his windows. Thieves have been tampering with the lawyer's windows. The lawyer advanced my brother the iron to make bars. My brother is excited. He will not make any money from this job for the lawyer, but the lawyer will be impressed by the quality of my brother's work. The lawyer will become a customer. Someday the lawyer will expand his practice and open offices in another building. The windows in that building will need bars, and my brother will make the bars for a good price.

We begin work immediately. It is late in the day to begin work. My brother works so fast that my arms begin to tremble. My brother works on and on. It is deafening in the forge. I begin to listen to the tapping and the clanging as though they are separate from our motions. They are sounds that come from the forge. My arms burn. They burn as though I have laid them on the hearth. I fall forward and put my face on the hearth. I see myself fall forward. I see myself fall past my brother. I see my brother's face as I fall past. My brother looks like our father, but then our father's face changed. He put his face on the hearth. On the hearth, coals burn through my nose. The fat in my lips bubbles out through the cracks. My eyelids puff out from my eyes. My brother drags me from the hearth. He lays me on my back on the floor. He douses my face with water from the slack tub. The water turns to steam. My eyes cook, my tongue cooks. I scream. I waver on my feet. The arm that holds the sledge falls down and the sledge misses the anvil. I take a step toward the hearth. I see myself fall forward. My brother catches me easily. I do not fall on the hearth. My brother catches me. He carries me through the double doors.

The sudden quiet feels like water in my ears, like someone has poured cold water in my ears. The wind is coming from the bay and the air outside the forge is sharp with salts. I twist my neck to look up past my brother's shoulder, at the moon. My brother's shoulder is a dark curve that covers half the sky but I can still see the hard light of the moon. I shut my eyes. The smell of my brother's sweat and the animal smell of the apron mingle with the salts from the bay. I am cradled against my brother's chest but I imagine I am inside the belly of a giant fish, swimming deeper and deeper in the dark water of the bay.

19

In the morning, I cannot remember how I got to my bed. The house smells good, like toasted bread. My brother is frying bread in butter in the pan. I eat the hot bread ravenously. Every muscle in my body aches. The calluses on my hands are cracked and they sting when I move my fingers. My brother says he will hire a helper, a boy to pump the bellows and sweep the floor. We will need a helper once we have the contract with the foreigners. He had better find a helper now. My brother goes down the path to the town. I stand in front of the forge and watch my brother walk down the path. Nothing blocks the sun and my brother's shadow is a dark bar on the grass. Once we have a contract with the foreigners, I will make my brother buy paint. I will paint ax handles. First I will paint the boards on either side of the windows in the front of the house. I will paint them yellow or blue.

Waiting for my brother, I fall asleep in the sun. When I wake up, my brother has returned from town with a boy. My brother does not look at me. He is embarrassed to see me stretched out sleeping in the sun. The boy does not look at me. He follows my brother into the forge. He is the same size as my brother, taller than my brother, but narrower than my brother, with narrow shoulders and a narrow head. His big hands dangle at his sides. I stand at the double doors. After lying in the sun, I can barely see the two dim figures in the forge. For a moment, I think that the figures are my brother and our father. The two figures move in the dimness of the forge. Then I remember there is a boy, a narrow-headed boy. He has come to be a helper, to help my brother and me, to perform the tasks that I will not have time to do.

My brother puts the iron on the hearth. The boy takes my position at the anvil. I wait for my brother to send the boy to the bellows. I wait for my brother to call me to the anvil. My brother calls to me. He does not turn his head. His back is to me. He faces the boy across the anvil. I do not see my brother's face but I hear what he calls. He has sent me to the bellows. I go to the bellows. I pump the bellows. I pump the bellows as fast as I can. My palms bleed. The fire in the hearth grows hotter and hotter. The iron on the hearth turns red. I do not stop. My brother and the striker work on and on. They stream with sweat. The din in the forge is louder than ever before.

When work stops for the day, my brother can speak. He does not look at me, but he speaks. The foreigners do not want my brother to repair the hardware for their ships. Instead, they have given my brother a contract for gates. He will make gates to enclose the foreign district of town. Too many townspeople are shopping in the foreign district of the town. It is more difficult for soldiers to recognize thieves when there are so many townspeople. The gates will help control access to the foreign district. Forging the gates is certain to be a very big job. With a reliable striker, my brother will not disappoint the foreigners. He will produce high-quality gates that the foreigners may open and close to control access to the foreign district. He will crown the gates with spikes. Climbing, the thieves will gouge their bodies on the spikes. Soldiers will remove those thieves who fail to extricate their bodies from the spikes. The foreign district will continue to expand. My brother will need to forge more and more gates. My brother could not have asked for a better contract from the foreigners.

My brother shows the striker to the bed. My brother tells the striker that I do not mind the pallet. I am happy to give the striker the bed. I do not mind the pallet. I am happy to give the striker the bed. When my brother pulls the pallet from beneath the bed, he gags. The pallet is white as though there were a clean sheet on the pallet. The sheet is composed of maggots, the many maggots that have hatched in the meat and the vomit I hid beneath the bed. The maggots wiggle on the pallet but the sound in the house is not the maggots. It is the sound of my brother holding back his vomit. I would laugh if my brother were to add his vomit to the vomit that produced the maggots. My brother does not vomit. He lets me push past him. I seize a corner of the pallet. I drag the pallet through the door and across the grass. Behind me I hear my brother stamping, crushing the maggots that dropped to the floor with his heels. I drag the pallet to the scrap pile behind the forge. I leave the pallet on the scrap pile. I lie down on the grass in front of the forge. The lights from the foreign district of the town are reflected on the waters of the bay.

20

I think that it is morning when I hear my brother coming toward me. He is ready to begin work in the forge. I open my
eyes and it is very dark. I smell the salty thickness of the fog,
the fog that hides the moon and the stars. It is not morning.
My back is stiff and wet. There is moisture on my face, moisture from the air. My brother wipes my face with his hands.
He pushes my hair. I close my eyes. I feel my brother lift my
head. He puts my head on his leg. He is sitting up beside me,
watching the dark fog, while I sleep against his leg. I want to
tell my brother to lie back, that we can both sleep on the grass
before the forge, but I cannot move my mouth. I cannot move
my head or my arms. My body is very heavy but my brother is
strong enough to bear my weight. He keeps pushing my hair,
and the pressure of the fog is warmer, and the droplets that
run on my body do not itch or tickle anymore. I let them run
over me.

The next time I open my eyes, it is morning. I sit up. Everything is dim, but there is a paleness at the edges, coming evenly from all directions. The fog is hanging just above the hill, thin and moon-colored, holding the same kind of light. My brother is sitting next to me. I look past him through the double doors of the forge, into the darkness of the forge. It is morning. We must begin work at the forge. My body is stiff from sleeping on the grass but I am ready to face my brother across the anvil. I remember that I am not my brother's striker. There is a boy in the bed in the house. He is waiting for my brother to wake him, to call him to his place at the anvil. I say my brother's name and he turns his face. I see his dark face in the light that comes from the fog. I pull the talisman from beneath my shirt. My brother's face darkens as he examines the misshapen iron. I untie the apron string and hold the talisman in my hand. It is a lump. No blacksmith would ever have forged such a lump. I throw the talisman away from the forge, down the hill. It is impossible to see where it lands through the fog. I give my brother the apron string and I open my pants. My hands are too small. They are not getting enough blood. There may be a blockage or there may be too much blood going somewhere else. The doctor said there was no blockage. Too much blood is going somewhere else.

I get up on my knees. I show my brother where the blood goes, how the blood goes too quickly away from my hands. My brother looks at the apron string in his hands. He does not look at me. I move closer. I lower my pants. My brother twists the apron string through his fingers. I take my brother's fingers and I move them toward me. The apron string drops and I drape it again through his fingers. I put his hand on me. When I let go, his hand falls away. He does not look at me. It is too hard to tie the knot myself, to pull it tight. I need my brother's help. How I can be my brother's striker if he refuses to do the thing that I need? There is moisture on my brother's face. His fingers are clumsy. The apron string burns then slackens. It falls on the grass. My brother has never failed to perform a task. He loops the apron string around me. The ends hang loose. My brother's hands dangle at his sides. He touches me but he does not tighten the strings. I feel the blood that follows his touch. I do not need my brother's touch. I need my brother to twist the strings tight. I need him to cut off the blood. He cannot fail to do this thing for me. It is good to have a brother for a striker. It is almost as good as having a son. I can be a son to my brother if he cuts off the blood. My hands will grow. I will be able to grip the sledge in my hands. My brother pulls the ends of the strings. He pulls the strings tight. He sits beside me. I put my head on his leg. The blood moves up. It moves up too slowly, but my brother waits. He will wait. He will hold my hands until they fill his grasp.